THE CRUISING FIASCO

A MCLAUGHLIN SISTERS NOVEL (STRANDED IN GETAWAY BAY ROMANCE, BOOK 3)

ELANA JOHNSON

ISBN-13: 978-1-63876-100-6

CHAPTER ONE

*O*rchid Stone stapled a packet of papers together, her thoughts on what she should make for dinner that night. She wondered if the other single women in the administration building at Petals & Leis had the same mundane thoughts she did.

She glanced around, though she only worked with three other people. They all looked as bored as she felt, and one of them really needed a boyfriend so they had something to talk about while they filed, answered phones, managed the huge orders that came in, and made sure everyone in the billion-dollar flower company got paid.

But yep, Orchid's life was very, very boring.

She had Tesla, her seven-year-old daughter who kept things hopping, but not during the day while she was at school. And today, Tesla had after-school activities at the recreation center in downtown Getaway Bay,

1

so Orchid wouldn't see her until after dinner, as her father was going to pick Tesla up on his way home from work and take her for something to eat.

Orchid's parents had been lifesavers since the boating accident that had claimed her husband eight years ago.

Eight long years.

She hadn't been on a date since the funeral.

"Jordyn," she said, getting up from her desk. "Didn't you meet someone on that app?"

The pretty brunette rolled her eyes, though Orchid had drawn the interest of the other two women in this part of the building. Cathy and Deirdre both got up and approached Jordyn's desk.

"It was awful," she said with tons of dramatic effect. Jordyn was the youngest in the office, and she'd been the most active on the dating scene. Orchid watched her, a smile on her face, as Jordyn opened a drawer and pulled out a file.

"Total surfer, despite me asking him—twice—if he surfed. And you know how I feel about pretty-boy surfers." She made a face, and Deirdre laughed.

"So he was pretty, then," Orchid said.

"Oh, so pretty." Jordyn smiled. "But I don't want someone whose whole goal in life is to catch the next wave. No. My husband will have ambition. Be someone."

"Sure," Deirdre said. "I'm just hoping for a date."

"There's that new speed dating thing coming up," Cathy said. "Have you girls heard of it?"

Jordyn shrieked, and Orchid was so glad she'd started this conversation. Anything was better than stapling together vendor packets for the carnation conference next week. Plus, once she finished that, she didn't have a whole lot to do.

Spring was a busy time out in the fields, but in the office, summer and fall and winter were definitely their busiest times.

"Orchid, could I see you a minute?" The voice came from her phone on her desk, and Orchid walked away from the conversation still going strong at Jordyn's desk.

"Yes, Mister Lawson," she said into the intercom. "I'll be right in." She wasn't worried or nervous. Burke Lawson was younger than her, and while he was set to inherit the entire operation one day, he hadn't done it yet. He did spend a lot of time consulting with his father, and George Lawson did inspire a bit of fear in Orchid.

So when she walked into Burke's office and found his father with him, she stalled. "Oh, hello, George." She closed the door behind her and fought the urge to smooth down her skirt. It suddenly felt too short and like it wasn't good enough as the two of them said hello and shook her hand.

She settled in the chair in front of Burke's desk, and he looked at his father, who nodded.

"Orchid, when's the last time you took a vacation day?"

She blinked, surprise rendering her silent.

"It's been over a year," Burke said for her, flipping open a folder. "You have eighty-four vacation days stockpiled." He closed the folder and smiled.

"I'm—am I in trouble for not taking time off?"

"Yes," he said. "You're a great employee, and we want you to be happy here."

"I am happy here," she said, looking back and forth between them. "Are you firing me?"

"Of course not." He chuckled and pushed the folder toward her. "But take a vacation, Orchid. You work too hard." He stood and smiled her right out of the office, leaving her more confused than ever—and now out of the loop in the conversation at Jordyn's desk.

Later that evening, she stopped by Ivy's apartment rather than facing her house alone. Tesla wouldn't be done with her granddad date for another couple of hours, and Orchid hated entering a dark, empty house by herself.

"There you are," Ivy said, opening the door before Orchid had finished climbing the steps. "What's this about a vacation?"

In response, Orchid practically threw the folder her boss had given her. "This is so stupid."

Ivy took the folder, clear amusement and bewilderment in her eyes, and opened it. A moment later, she sucked in a breath. "Orchid, are you going to do this

4

singles cruise? I've always wanted to go on one of these." She danced in front of Orchid, everything sparkling in her now.

Orchid worked hard not to roll her eyes. "Of course I'm not," she said. "A singles cruise? I can't imagine anything more demeaning. And the fact that my *boss* gave me that pamphlet? *Humiliating.*" She sank onto the couch, wondering where her afternoon had gone. Once she'd gotten the folder and opened it, all she'd been able to do was stare.

Ivy giggled and flipped pages. "They do fun things on these cruises, Orchid. You should totally go."

"Who would watch Tesla?"

"Uh, Mom and Dad," she said. "Eden. Now that she's married, she certainly doesn't need to work. Heaven knows she could take a break from that shed where she's always tinkering."

"I don't want to go on a singles cruise," she said.

"Uh, holy sharks and pearls, Orchid. Did you see this?" She lifted a piece of paper out of the folder.

Orchid had not made it past the first page. "What is that?"

"It's a certificate," she said, her eyes scanning the page. "This cruise is paid for." She exploded to her feet. "Holy shipwrecks, Orchid." Ivy's eyes met Orchid's, and the excitement there was undeniable. "It's. *Paid. For.*"

Orchid couldn't believe it. "That can't be true." She snatched the paper from Ivy, who started hopping around like someone had poured hot ants in her pants. She read the paper too, and sure enough, it certainly looked like she could book a two-week singles cruise free of charge.

"Wow." She lowered the paper, so many emotions battling inside her. "Doesn't mean I have to go."

"Oh, you're going." Ivy took the paper back and pressed it to her chest as if in bliss. Her eyes snapped open. "If you don't want it, can I have it?"

Something about that irked Orchid, and she took the paper and the folder back. "No, Ivy. You're dating Brooks, and he's going to propose any day now. You can't go on a singles cruise."

"I've always wanted to go," she said, a whine in her voice.

"Tell me why," Orchid said, glancing at the closed folder on the couch beside her. She couldn't really go on a singles cruise. Could she?

Ivy started talking about how "super fun" they were, with "all the activities" they planned for people. "It's so much more than laying by the pool," she said. "They have themed cruises, and dances, and trivia, and paint nights." She sighed. "You really should go. I can't believe I haven't suggested this to you before."

Orchid could. She'd made it clear to her sisters that she wasn't interested in dating. Period. The end.

But if she went on a singles cruise, wouldn't that be like dating? Why had her boss given this to her?

Ivy kept talking, as Ivy was wont to do, and Orchid

pulled out her phone and texted Burke. *You gave me a singles cruise? What are you trying to say?*

A singles cruise? His response did not inspire confidence in her. *I don't think so.*

There's a certificate for a singles cruise in that folder you gave me, she typed out, her thumbs moving like lightning over her screen. *What does that mean?*

She hoped she sounded offended and angry, and she must have, because Burke called.

"Yeah?" she answered, not even caring that the word came out like a bark.

"That was an honest mistake," Burke said instead of leading with hello. "I said we should give a few of our hardest working employees a bonus. We looked up who hadn't taken time off in a while, and your name came up. My father said he'd get vacations for each of you, and I didn't think twice about it."

"Who else got one of these?" Orchid asked.

"Leslie in accounting," Burke said, gasping in the next moment. "Lizzie in maintenance. She's married."

Orchid started laughing, and Burke joined in. "I'm sure my father didn't know what he was buying. What's the name of the cruise line?"

"StarMatch," Orchid said, their horrible logo branded on the backs of her eyes.

"It was an innocent mistake," Burke said. "I'll see what I can do about it in the morning. Unless, of course, you want to go on a singles cruise...."

Orchid didn't know what she wanted. She ended up

telling Burke she'd let him know, and she hung up. Turning, she caught Ivy saying, "Yes, of course. Eight a.m. on Thursday. She'll be there."

She hung up the phone too, and when she looked at Orchid, Orchid knew exactly what had just happened.

THURSDAY CAME, and Orchid kissed her daughter good-bye while Ivy took her suitcase out to the car. She'd tried everything she could to get out of the cruise, but once Ivy had booked it, Burke couldn't get his money back.

"It'll be good for you," Ivy had said in the three days since turning Orchid's life upside down.

"You need this." That was another one her sister had said several times.

Even Eden and Iris had gotten behind the idea of a singles cruise. Eden had come over last night and packed a backpack for Orchid with all the emergency supplies she'd need. She'd hugged her sister and told her to have fun.

Iris had sent her a list of ways to flirt with a winky face, and Orchid had been mortified. Her sisters knew what she'd been through. They knew she hadn't dated in eight long years. They knew her better than anyone.

And that alone was what had her boarding the ship along with twenty-five other thirty-and-flirty-somethings, her flip flops pinching between her toes.

Orchid had a hard time determining age when she looked at the men and women already onboard. She certainly felt older than all of them, and she wondered if any of them had children. Had been married before. Had buried a spouse.

Her emotions spiraled, but she put on a smile, the way Ivy had told her to. She turned toward the closest man, determined to talk to him. That way, when Ivy messaged her and asked her how things were going, Orchid could say she'd at least tried.

Maybe that was all she needed to do. Try.

"Hey," she said to the impossibly tall man in front of her. His brown hair seemed like it needed a cut, but the shaggy locks looked good on him. He wore a full beard too, and Orchid tried not to swoon.

So maybe this would be good for her.

"My name's Orchid," she said, finally drawing the man's attention to her.

He didn't smile. Didn't even act like he heard her. Maybe he hadn't. He was quite a bit taller than her. Wider.

Another blonde joined them, creating a little triangle. She also wore little triangles of fabric over her private parts—and not much else. "Hey," she said. "I'm Amber."

"Maine," the man said, and it seemed like every female on the ship flocked toward him then.

Orchid took a step back, disgusted by him. He couldn't even acknowledge that she'd spoken to him? Sure, maybe she wasn't as pretty and perky as Amber, but she had a cute swimming suit on too—underneath her clothes.

"Jerk," she muttered, deciding to get out of the sun for a little bit. She didn't have to tell Ivy she'd only tried one conversation.

She'd tried—and that was more than she'd done in eight years.

As she locked herself in her room, she couldn't help feeling like this singles cruise was a bad, bad idea.

CHAPTER TWO

*M*aine Fitzgerald cursed himself the moment his name slipped from his mouth. He hadn't been planning to use it, though he suspected some people on the cruise would recognize him. He was the starting quarterback for the Getaway Bay Orcas, after all.

He glanced around for his buddy, Shane Sanders, who played wide receiver. But the guy couldn't be found. He was probably off with someone he'd just met already, and Maine cursed himself for agreeing to this stupid cruise in the first place.

Almost immediately, he eradicated the thought. He'd wanted to come too. The traditional dating scene on the island wasn't working for him, and he'd heard good things about StarMatch. They had good, clean fun, and while they didn't guarantee anything, he knew a few people had found a long-lasting relationship on the cruise.

Maine couldn't believe it, but he wanted a long-lasting relationship for himself. Since coming to the island of Getaway Bay and becoming the starting quarterback for the Orcas, he'd been striking out left and right. And he wasn't even playing baseball.

He'd been out with four women in a couple of years, and he'd had feelings for each of them. But the pouty, flirty blonde in front of him was exactly like Louise, and Maine had learned how to read the signs of a woman who wanted arm candy and not much more.

Well, Maine was tired of being a showpiece. He wanted someone he could be real with. Someone he could share his dreams with. He knew he wasn't going to play professional football forever, and he had more in mind for his life.

He watched a beautiful blonde back away from him, her face forming into a scowl before she turned and left. He wasn't sure why she'd done that, but he also couldn't chase after her. Instead, he edged away from the woman who was probably a decade younger than him, unsure of what she'd said her name was. He couldn't exactly hear very well, but he'd told his mother he was only thirty-one years old, and he was not wearing hearing aids unless he was on the field. Then, he had to be able to hear.

But on a singles cruise, he didn't. Behind him, music blared, and he turned in that direction, wishing this mix and mingle would end and the more structured games and activities would begin. He'd never been great at making small talk, unless he could talk about a long pass or the formation he liked best with his offensive linemen.

He caught sight of Shane, who had a woman on either side of him. Shane didn't even look in Maine's direction, though the men were tall enough to see over the heads of those around them.

He tuned in to the conversation beside him, glad there was another man there carrying it. He was tall, with a lot of hair on top of his head, the sides shaved. He had a big, bright, white smile, and a lot of the women were watching him.

"Cal," he said to another woman, and everyone looked at Maine.

"Maine," he said, glad the guy before him had established that last names were not needed.

"You're Maine Fitzgerald," a woman said, this one with long auburn hair that flipped around in the breeze.

"Yes," he said, glancing at Cal. Could this guy save him the way Shane would've?

"You're Maine Fitzgerald?" Cal said, leaning forward. "It *is* Maine Fitzgerald."

Maine put a smile on his face, because that was what he'd been trained to do. He had a legit public relations specialist and everything. He met with Clarissa before every game, and for at least ten minutes before he went out and faced the press after every game. He sat through lessons on how to act on the way to practice and on the way home, how to deal with fans at the grocery store, all of it.

Maine had stopped doing his own shopping long ago, thanks to apps and websites and delivery services. But he did still go out in public, and he didn't mind the attention. Usually.

Today, though, he wished he were with the curvy blonde walking away from him as fast as she could.

He answered questions, and eventually Shane came and got him, saying, "Dude, I need you for a minute. I need him, guys."

Maine walked away with his best friend amidst murmurs of, "That's Shane Sanders," and "How many of them are on this cruise?"

"What's going on?" Maine asked.

"Nothing," Shane said. "You looked like you could use some help."

"Thanks." Maine glanced over his shoulder to the crowd. Only a couple of people were still watching him and Shane, and Maine figured the hype about their presence would die down soon enough. He hoped so. He didn't want to be famous for the next two weeks.

"Drink up," Shane said when they reached the smoothie station. "Training starts in two weeks, and then we'll be off sugar."

Maine groaned just thinking about it. He sure had enjoyed the absence of his physical trainer the past couple of months. He worked out on his own, but he relaxed a bit with his diet. Not so during the training season, preseason, and then regular season, when he had to be in top mental and physical condition.

"Mango pineapple strawberry," he said to the bartender. "Virgin, please." He didn't drink, even during off-season, and Shane didn't either. Maine needed all of his brain cells, and he'd seen some guys do really stupid things while intoxicated. He didn't want to jeopardize his career in that way, and he'd found he could enjoy the cocktails without alcohol as well as with.

A minute later, he stepped away from the bar with his tall glass rimmed with sugar, scanning for a group to belong to. He couldn't identify one immediately, so he detoured over to a lounger and sat down. He didn't need to talk or be part of a group all the time.

He enjoyed the breeze, the scent of suntan lotion and fruit hanging in the air, the laughter and vibrancy surrounding him. A while later, just as he finished his drink, an announcement blared through the speakers on the ship.

"Make your way to the game room, where a rousing game of Battle of the Sexes Trivia will begin in five minutes."

Maine stood up, ready to have some fun on this cruise. He and Shane followed the signs to the game room, which was down one level and on the back of the ship, with another pool on the other side of the wall of windows.

Only about a dozen people had shown up for Battle of the Sexes Trivia, and Maine noticed the blonde that had walked away from him earlier. She wore a one-piece swimming suit now, her regular clothes gone. The suit only had one strap, and Maine stared at her bare shoulder for a moment too long.

Realizing what he was doing, he cleared his throat and edged away from her and toward the rest of the men in the room.

"Seven men, five women," the coordinator said as if the rest of the adults in the room couldn't count. "Two women will have to go twice. Okay? Here we go!" She smiled as if they'd win money in this trivia game, and Maine decided now was the time to have some fun.

He stepped up to the table first amidst cheers from the other men there. To his great astonishment, the blonde he'd ogled joined him, a fierce look of determination on her face.

"In golf," the coordinator read in a very game-show host type of voice. "A bogey means... one: one under par. Two: par. Three: one over par. Four: two over par."

Lightning fast, the woman's hand smacked the buzzer in front of her. "Three: one over par."

"Correct!" the coordinator bellowed, and all the women cheered. Maine cocked his eyebrows at her, because she did not look like the type to be on the golf course on a regular basis.

He stepped back, bowing his head as a smile crossed her face. "What's your name?" he asked.

"I already told you once today," she said, giving him a *so-there* look before turning back to her team, who were now all her best friends as they hugged and high-fived. He waited his turn, his eyes never straying far from the woman who said she'd told him her name.

She hadn't. Had she? Maybe that was why she'd scowled at him and stomped off. She'd introduced herself and he hadn't heard her.

He had to know her name before they left this tournament.

The score volleyed back and forth, until finally, he faced her again on the final point. The coordinator, a woman who wore a nametag that read Jessie, looked back and forth between them.

"How many weeks is the typical pregnancy?"

Orchid grinned wickedly at him, and Maine felt something shift inside him. He had no idea, but it was clear he could've at least guessed. He didn't. Orchid hit the buzzer and said, "Two: forty," with supreme confidence.

"And the women win!" Jessie said, throwing her cards up in the air as if the women in the room had just won an all-expenses-paid trip to Paris. Or somewhere women liked to go.

Most of the other men started shuffling out of the room while the women celebrated, but Maine hung back. He had to know who this woman was, as her soul seemed to be calling to his in a way no one's had before.

"Congrats," he said once she'd finished celebrating. He extended his hand for her to shake. "Would you mind telling me your name again? Things were loud on the boat earlier, and I...." He glanced around and the few women still loitering nearby. "I have some hearing damage, and I refuse to wear hearing aids."

Her eyebrows shot up. "Is that so? Or did you just make that up, because you're embarrassed I spoke to you and you ignored me?"

"I didn't hear you," he said, feeling a twist of guilt move through him. "Honestly, I didn't."

She cocked one delicious hip, and if she didn't tell him her name, Maine would do whatever it took to learn it for himself. "I'm Maine Fitzgerald," he said, waiting for the light of recognition to flood her eyes.

It didn't.

And dang if that didn't make her more attractive to him.

"Fine," she said, a flirty smile finally touching her mouth. "I'm Orchid Stone." She shook his hand, and a zing shot all the way up to Maine's shoulder.

"Nice to meet you," he said, hoping he could spend a lot of the next two weeks with this woman.

She started for the exit, and he fell into step beside her. He wasn't sure what the next activity was, but wherever Orchid went, Maine would just go there too.

"I'm surprised you didn't know the golf question,"

she said. "What with you being a big sports star and all."

He paused, his pulse thundering through him. So she did know who he was—and she just didn't care.

She giggled as she flipped that long, blonde hair over her shoulder and walked away. He'd seen her do that once before, and her hips seriously hadn't had that sway last time.

"I knew the golf question," he called after her, but she just lifted her hand in a wave as if it didn't matter. "I did," he muttered to himself.

He didn't care that she'd walked away from him, or that she'd beaten him at the trivia game. No, all he cared about was finding her again and learning more about her.

"Orchid Stone," he said, a smile crossing his face with the name.

"Are you doing the mile walk?" Jessie asked. "The first ten get a free T-shirt."

"Where's that?" he asked, his eyes still on Orchid's back.

"The track," Jessie said. "The upper deck. There's a pizza party afterward."

"Thanks," Maine said, noticing that Orchid had started up the steps. He didn't want to stalk her, but he could definitely use a long walk and a piece of pizza.

And Orchid Stone in his life.

CHAPTER THREE

*O*rchid didn't particularly want to participate in the mile walk. But Ivy had told her to "get out there and do everything." It wouldn't be a vacation if she did what she always did. Sit around. Wish for something more in her life.

So Orchid had put on the flirty swimming suit her sister had insisted she take. She'd gone to Battle of the Sexes Trivia, and she wasn't disappointed to see the tall, tan football player there. Surprised, yes. But not disappointed.

And beating him? Even better.

A smile curved her lips, and she went up another flight of stairs to the top deck. She moved out of the way so those behind her could get to the track too, but she kept a tight hold on the railing there, a sense of vertigo overcoming her.

"Are you okay?" That delicious voice purred in her

ear, and she blinked as she turned her head to see who it was.

Maine Fitzgerald.

Her fingers ached, but Orchid didn't dare let go. "I have a bit of a phobia of heights," she whispered before she could tell him to get lost.

"I'm sorry?" he asked, leaning down. Oh, so he was going to perpetuate the utter lie that he couldn't hear.

"Dude," another man said, slapping Maine on the back. "Get hearing aids already. The only person you're hurting is yourself." The dark-haired man grinned like a fool, his gaze finally sliding to Orchid. "Oh, hello. Who do we have here?"

Maine inched toward her, partially blocking her from the wide receiver Shane Sanders. "She's with me," Maine said, almost possessively.

Orchid wasn't sure if she liked it or not. "I'm Orchid Stone," she said, very loudly and very clearly.

Shane blinked at her, that playboy smile hitched in place. "I'm not the deaf one, sweetheart." He clapped Maine on the shoulder. "Good to meet you. Seems like you and Maine have stuff to talk about." He walked away, joining another group of singles and starting around the track.

Orchid watched them go, aware that Maine was looking at her and not his friend. She finally allowed herself to look at him, pure humiliation pulling through her. "So I guess you really are hard of hearing."

22

Flames touched his cheeks, and he looked away. "A little. It's nothing really."

"I'm afraid of heights," she said, forcing herself not to look down. "That's what I said a minute ago." At least things had stopped spinning now. "I think...." She uncurled her fingers from the railing and took a step toward the track. Then another one. A third, and she thought she might actually be able to walk up there while the boat moved below her.

The thought sent her reeling again, and Maine grabbed onto her hand with his, grounding her.

A shower of sparks moved through her, and she couldn't help leaning into that tall, strong body for extra support. Wow, he smelled amazing, like cologne, and male skin, and suntan lotion.

"Maybe we should just go sit by the pool," he said.

"Maybe," she agreed, and she let him lead her back to the steps and down them to the main deck. Things didn't seem to move quite so violently here, and she glanced up to the top deck where the track sat. "I guess exercising on this cruise is out."

"Hey, it's vacation," Maine said. "No exercise needed."

"You can go back up," she said. "I don't want to keep you from your activities."

"I'm fine here," he said, his fingers tightening along hers for a moment before releasing.

She stared at her hand, as if just now realizing it was attached to her body and that Maine had been touching it. "I don't actually exercise at home either," she said stupidly. She tried to suck the words back in, but they were already out. Ivy would be so disappointed in Orchid.

Maine just chuckled and pointed toward the end of the pool. "There's a pizza party later, but maybe you'd like to get a drink and just talk?"

Orchid would like that, but she couldn't believe Maine wanted to do anything of the sort, at least with her. But then he had his hand in hers again, and he was moving toward the snack bar. So she went with him. Ordered what she wanted. Followed him to a couple of open loungers beneath an umbrella.

He sighed as he sat down, and she noticed the way he favored his right leg. "Is that from the injury at the end of last season?" she asked.

His eyes flew to hers. "I'm fine."

"I know," she said. "I just thought—never mind." She sipped her drink, cursing herself for asking such a bold question. "How do you like Getaway Bay?"

"It's nice," he said. So much for the talking part. He just sucked on his straw and stared out at the people in the pool.

"Do you have a boyfriend?" Maine asked, and Orchid slowly moved her eyes back to his.

"What? It's a *singles* cruise. Did you not get that memo?" She grinned at him, glad when he chuckled.

"So no boyfriend," he said.

"No," she confirmed. "Do you have a girlfriend?"

She glanced around. "Maybe someone already here. Are you here with someone, Maine?" She put plenty of theatrics into her voice so he'd know she was teasing him.

But Orchid couldn't believe she was teasing him. She didn't tease, or flirt, or even know how to talk to a man. Not only that, but this was a man among men, being the starting quarterback for the Orcas. He was a legend around town, and everyone loved him. Absolutely everyone.

If her sister knew who she was talking to…or her father. Orchid smiled to herself, almost desperate to get back to her phone in her room.

"I'm not here with anyone," he said with a smile. "Except that guy who tried to steal you away from me. Shane."

"Right," she said. "Wide receiver."

"How do you know so much about football?" he asked.

"I know enough," Orchid said, not wanting to tell him her husband's favorite sport was football, and she'd picked up a few things from the dozens and dozens of games they'd watched together. "How long have you played?"

"My whole life," he said, the wind picking up and tossing his hair around.

Behind her, the loudspeaker crackled, and the normally jovial voice that had been announcing the activities said, "Ladies and gentlemen, we need everyone to gather in the Level Two conference room immediately. I repeat, please leave your rooms and activities and go straight to the Level Two conference room. Faculty and staff, this is a code white."

"Code white?" Orchid asked, glancing around.

Maine stood up and extended his hand to her. "Let's go."

"You're just going to go?"

A woman went running by them, wearing the official uniform of a StarMatch employee. "Everyone inside now!" she yelled, and Orchid didn't miss the urgency in her voice.

"Yep," Maine said. "*We're* going to go."

She kept her hand tucked in his as he led her toward the steps and down two levels to a conference room. Everyone wearing a blue polo with the Star-Match logo on it looked like they were about to throw up, and Orchid asked three of them what a code white was before she realized they weren't going to tell her.

"We deserve to know," she said as Maine entered the conference room. They were in the first half of people to arrive, and Orchid folded her arms and watched the muscular men in black polos do the same.

Something was definitely going down. At first, she'd thought the ship was sinking.

Don't be ridiculous, she told herself, wishing she'd run to her room really quick to get her backpack of supplies. Eden had given her so much more than she'd sent with Iris, and it was only because of her sister's time on a deserted island that Orchid was even thinking abandoning ship was an option.

Of course, Henry's boat had sunk too.

She shivered, and Maine glanced down at her. "You okay?"

She shook her head, tears springing to her eyes instantly. She hated this weakness inside her, but she hadn't found a way to root it out and get rid of it yet. She simply lived with the anxiety, the tremors shaking her stomach, her lungs, the back of her tongue.

"Is everyone here?" someone asked, and several radios chirped and the same message came through all of them.

"Final sweep," the man making the announcements said. "We have two minutes. Get to a secure position."

One of the black-shirted men climbed on a table and bellowed, "I need everyone to be quiet so I can count." He started tapping his finger in mid-air as he moved in a slow circle as he counted. "All twenty-six are here," he said into the radio on his hip.

Orchid's second idea that perhaps someone on the ship had been hurt vanished. If they were all in the room, that obviously wasn't true. Maybe someone had had something stolen.

"Copy that. Inform," came through the radio.

"Ladies and gentlemen," he said, as the other man dressed like him moved to the door and latched it. "We need to stay calm. You are in the safest room on the ship."

"Why do we need to be in here?" a man called out.

A very good question, in Orchid's opinion.

"There was an earthquake out in the ocean," the man said, his delivery smooth and flawless. "There's a tsunami headed for our ship."

CHAPTER FOUR

*L*ike the dozens of people around Maine, his first thought was to pull out his phone and call for help. He did, his phone always just a reach away in his back pocket, except when he was out on the field.

"No service," he said at the same time Orchid sucked in a tight breath and held it.

"I need my backpack," she said, every syllable full of panic.

Maine looked at her, actually watching the color drain from her face. "Is there medicine in there you need?" he asked, looking at the beefy guy on the table. He could probably take him in an open area, but not in here. Not when he was up there.

"Calm down," he shouted. "The ship won't capsize."

"He doesn't know that," Orchid said, bracing her

hands on her knees and sucking at the air. "My husband's yacht wasn't supposed to be able to capsize either. Had the...technology...still...went...under...."

By the end of her sentence, Maine couldn't really make out the words. Her voice went in and out like she was losing reception.

He put his hand on her back and said, "It's okay, Orchid. Just breathe."

She did, the swell of her back against his palm comforting.

"The wave is going to hit us in thirty seconds," the man said. He got down off the table. "I want as many people under the table as will fit, and—"

No one waited for the rest of the instructions, Maine included. He pushed Orchid under the table, as she was the closest one to it. "Scoot in, Orchid," he said. "As far as you can."

Cries and gasps and general anxiety filled the air. Maine was used to a high-pressure situation, but this was a little different than trying to find the open receiver forty yards down the field.

He managed to fold his tall frame in half and slide under the table beside Orchid. She had her eyes closed, and she sat cross-legged under the very center of the table. He crowded in beside her so someone else could have the edge of the space remaining.

Maine looked around, trying to find Shane. He had to be here. Everyone was accounted for, right?

"Hold on," the man yelled, and Maine grabbed one

of the table legs, reaching right over another woman's head to do it.

In the next moment, the boat swung wildly. Screams filled the air, and Maine wasn't entirely sure he hadn't added to chaos. Orchid definitely had, and she cried openly now. With his other arm, he gathered her right against his chest.

"It's—" Another violent sway in the opposite direction stole the word "okay" from his throat. She clung to him now, and Maine didn't mind. If he could help her, he would. He'd heard her say something about her husband's boat going under, and he couldn't imagine what fresh nightmare she was living.

The ship groaned, a deep guttural noise that didn't inspire confidence. "What is that?" someone asked, their voice full of alarm.

"We're evening out," the man said, but in the next moment, the ship lurched again. Knees and elbows hit Maine in the back and sides, and he jabbed other people too. Someone screamed, and another woman said, "She's out from underneath the table!"

The boat continued to sway and swing, until finally, the motion stopped.

Maine didn't dare move. What if this was like an earthquake, where there could still be aftershocks? Did that happen with tsunamis? He'd grown up in Texas, and he knew hardly anything about earthquakes. Hurricanes, sure.

Silence descended upon the room, except for a little

bit of residual crying and sniffling. Orchid was utterly silent and if not for the way she had her arms cinched around Maine's torso, he'd have thought her dead or asleep.

"It's okay to come out now," the man said. "We've already radioed for a rescue boat, but it'll be morning before they get here."

Maine waited his turn while others slid and shuffled out from underneath the table. He pulled Orchid with him, keeping her tight against his side. "It's okay," he said to her. "We're okay. There's food on the ship, and we'll be fine until help arrives."

Several others looked at him too, and he decided if he had to be the voice of comfort, so be it. The security guard repeated the same things he did, and his partner released them from the room.

"Ladies and gentlemen," came over the loud-speaker, and Orchid flinched. Maine too was triggered, as now he knew what damage could come from an announcement. "Your attention please. We've lost both our engines. We won't be able to continue on this boat. Rest assured, our rescue vessel will be here in the morning, and we have plenty of water and food."

So everything Maine had just said was really true. "All right," he said to Orchid. "Let's go get that back-pack, just in case. Okay?" He held her at arm's length, and looking into those gorgeous, if not a little watery, blue eyes, he could see her strength. See her phantoms.

"Okay," she said, and Maine let her direct him to her cabin.

———

THAT NIGHT, THE PARTY ATMOSPHERE ON THE boat seemed to have returned, at least a little bit. Maine ate a lot of pizza, figuring he wasn't sure when or where his next meal would come from so he should get as full as possible.

Orchid stayed at his side, and Maine managed to carry on a conversation with her about surface things. She'd told him about her three sisters, two of whom had been in the news in the past couple of years as they'd been stranded in remote locations.

That's not going to happen to us, he told himself. Number one, there were fifty people on this ship, and they had working communications. Number two, there were no islands in sight, but he wasn't sure if that was comforting or not. And third, Orchid had an entire backpack of emergency supplies. Maine wanted to go to his cabin and pack something similar, but he didn't have a utility knife, or unbreakable cords, or a desalination kit. He could bring extra clothes, but he was sure they wouldn't do much against the endless ocean beyond the ship.

Shane had found him soon after they'd been released from the conference room on Level Two, and they'd stuck together. Night fell, but Maine didn't want to go to his room. Eventually, the security team on the ship came around and told everyone to go to their cabins, and Maine went with Orchid to hers before following Shane to his.

Maine was right next door, and he said, "See you on the flip side," to his buddy before going inside and closing the door behind him. He did a thorough search of his room and found a life vest under the cushion of the desk chair. He strapped it around himself and fell onto the narrow bed.

Just in case, he thought as his exhaustion overwhelmed him and he fell asleep.

He woke when he fell out of bed. A curse sat at the tip of his tongue—until he remembered the events of the previous afternoon. Then panic coated everything, and he pushed himself to his feet and flew out the door.

People ran by him, screaming from somewhere in the distance. But the biggest problem in Maine's opinion, was the driving rain on the deck outside his door.

He was soaked in a matter of seconds, and still his only thought was to get to Orchid and make sure she was okay. It was insane, really. He'd only known the woman for a day, and yet he felt a connection to her. He'd wanted to get to know her before the tsunami, and that hadn't changed. He also felt the insane need to keep her safe. Protect her. Make sure nothing bad happened to her, as it had obviously happened to her husband.

Husband.

She was definitely older like him, and he wondered how long she'd been married. What exactly had happened. And if she had kids.

He wasn't going to ask her any of those things until later. Much later. Maybe when they made it back to dry land and he asked her to dinner.

An announcement came over the speaker system, but it only broadcast every other word, and Maine had no idea what they were saying. He finally moved, running and slipping as he headed toward Orchid's cabin.

He saw employees directing people toward the back of the boat, where he caught sight of another ship thrashing in the weather. The very bad, very tropical-storm-like weather.

The wind howled and rain pounded his shoulders. Men opened their mouths, but he couldn't hear the sound of their yells above the thunder and power of Mother Nature. This was very, very bad.

Maine found Orchid cowering in the door, her backpack on and her face full of fright. "Come on," he said, grabbing her hand. "We have to get on the other ship." He towed her after him, slowing down now so they both didn't land flat on their faces.

The press of people had dwindled from what he'd

caught sight of a few minutes ago, but the other ship heaved away from the one he and Orchid were still on. People swayed and fell, cries lifting into the air, where the waves smothered them.

The two ships moved closer together again, and several more people made it from the limping boat to the new one. "That's it!" a man yelled on the other side of the tumultuous ocean. "No more. We're going to tear in half!"

"No," Maine said, nowhere near loud enough for anyone to hear him. "They can't leave." He couldn't stay on this boat. This dead-in-the-water boat, going nowhere but underwater.

One security guard remained on the ship, as well as the captain and two other singles. And Maine and Orchid. It was only six more people.

The ship beneath him groaned again, and Maine rushed toward the railing. "Let us come over!" He waved his arms above his head, feeling his feet slip out from underneath him. He landed hard on the deck, stars shooting behind his eyes and up into his brain.

He struggled to stand up, but he managed to do it. He felt like he'd just been sacked by the biggest defensive lineman in the football association. "Please," he said. "We can't survive over here."

He got pulled back, and then he had no choice as the other boat backed away, slowly getting obscured by the waves and surf and wind and rain.

His only chance of getting to safety, just fading before his very eyes.

Cold fingers slipped into his, and then Orchid's pretty face loomed in front of his. "Come on, Maine," she said. "We have to ride out the storm down below."

CHAPTER FIVE

*O*rchid huddled with Maine at her side, an eternal chill inside her again. She'd felt like this after finding out Henry had passed away. *Lost at sea* was the term the Coast Guard had used, and Orchid never did get to see her husband again.

The thoughts of him out there in the ocean, somewhere, had haunted her for months. Even now, she couldn't stop thinking about it.

The remaining people on the boat sat in the conference room, saying nothing.

If only she hadn't frozen in her doorway. Then she could've been one of the earlier people in line to move from the bad ship to the working one. As it was, she'd had to wait for Maine to show up, and the weakness inside her seemed to grow and bloom, staining everything.

The ship lurched, and a massive, metal-on-metal

sound met her ears. The captain scrambled to his feet only moments before he started sliding away from where Maine and Orchid sat against the wall.

"Get to a lifeboat!" he yelled, his last word getting swallowed by the mechanical screaming still filling the air. Maine grabbed Orchid's hand and they ran from the room. She couldn't breathe, and she couldn't really feel her feet, but she managed to move.

The ship tipped dangerously, and Maine yelled, "Hold on!" and he got to work untying a boat. The security guard appeared at her side, practically pinning her to the railing. He helped Maine with the front of the lifeboat, and together, they got it lowered into the frothing water below.

"We have to get away from the ship," the security guard yelled, and Maine grabbed Orchid and swung over the side of the boat with all the athleticism she'd expect from a starting quarterback in the NFL.

She screamed into the weeping sky, finally hitting the hard surface of the boat. Maine reached up and helped the security guard down, calling, "Anyone else?"

No one appeared, and the security guard took the life jacket from Orchid, and he and Maine sat in the middle of the boat, manning the oars.

"Away from the ship," the security guard said, and Maine repeated it. Over and over, with every stroke.

Orchid didn't feel seconds away from getting ripped in half the further from the boat they moved, and a mild sense of relief wound through her. The rain lessened and lessened until it finally subsided too.

Then they were left alone with soaking wet clothes, the three of them in a lifeboat, and miles and miles of water in every direction.

"I'M TANNER," THE SECURITY GUARD SAID sometime later. Orchid didn't know how much time had passed. Could've been minutes or hours. She honestly wasn't sure.

"Orchid," she said.

"Maine." He stared lifelessly out into the water, and Orchid wanted to snap her fingers in front of his face and tell him to focus. Get them somewhere safe, where they could find food and build a shelter.

"Okay," she said, when neither man said another word. She could boss them around. She did it all day and all night, whether she wanted to or not. She put on her Mom-pants and said, "Let's think. Which way was the ship going when we hit the tsunami?"

"Our singles cruises go out to the north," Tanner said. "For three days. Then we circle back around Maui, and all the way down and around Getaway Bay again on the Big Island."

"So we're north of the Big Island," she said. "We moved all day."

"Right," Tanner said.

41

"There are islands out here," Orchid said, sending up a prayer that the wind would stop altogether. Her clothes were soaked, and she shivered. "Did either of you read about the couples that got stranded on the same island over and over?"

Maine looked as blank as ever, and Tanner shook his head.

Orchid worked hard not to roll her eyes. "Well, I read about them, and I know there are islands out here." She peered into the same distance Maine was looking. "So we just need to find one, and then we'll wait for help to come."

"Do you think help is coming?" Maine asked.

"Of course," Orchid said, glad some of her earlier shock and fear had worn off. It seemed to have been transferred right into Maine, as he continued to stare catatonically at the horizon.

The sky held an ominous shade of gray, but no more rain fell. Several minutes later, the sun broke through, and Orchid peered up at it. "Do you think that's east? It was morning when the other ship arrived, right?"

"It's almost nine o'clock now," Tanner said, glancing at Maine. He nudged him with his shoulder, and that seemed to bring the football player back to life.

"So yes," Tanner added. "That's east."

"Seems like I read that the islands were north and a bit west of the main island," Orchid mused. She looked behind the two men in the boat, but she couldn't see the Big Island, of course. A slip of foolishness pulled through her, and she faced what she believed to be north again. "So let's just keep going this way."

"You really think there will be islands out here?" Maine asked. "With a storm surge and a tsunami? They could be submerged."

Submerged.

Fear gripped Orchid's heart with that single word. "True," she said. "What ideas do you guys have? Can we go south? We'll run into the Big Island then, right?"

"No way," Tanner said. "The waves are too powerful to row against. We have to go with the waves until the storm is completely gone." He nodded toward the southern sky. "And it's not."

Orchid drew in a deep breath. "Okay. Go with the waves, but let's keep looking for any sign of land." She felt like an idiot for stating the obvious, but both men agreed, and she went back to scanning the ocean waves for any hint of green among so much blue.

HOURS LATER, ORCHID FELT SURE HER stomach would claw itself out for want of food. She'd gone through her backpack a half a dozen times, and Eden had packed plenty to eat. But Orchid had no way of knowing how long she'd be without food, which made rationing impossible.

Tears gathered in her eyes, but she pushed them back. She would not cry in front of these two men, one of whom she'd just started to like. She couldn't help the thoughts of Henry, as no one seemed to feel much like talking, and she'd been left to her own mind.

"Right there," Maine said, standing up and disturbing the equilibrium in the boat. "There's an island right over there." He pointed due east, and Orchid followed his outstretched arm.

"Oh, wow," she said, startled at how close it was. "Why didn't we see that?" The pale sand shone in the sun like gold now, and all the trees were the purest of greens.

"Doesn't matter," Tanner said, positioning himself at the oars. "Let's get this boat out of the water." He heaved against the waves, lining the boat up with the island, which had some rocky cliffs on one side. The articles she'd read about the prior strandings spoke of a cave the couples had used for shelter, but these cliffs looked a little too jagged for such things.

Tanner groaned and grunted, and he still couldn't get them all the way to the beach before he stood and said, "Maine, you take us in."

Maine put his hands on the oars, and while each stroke wasn't as powerful as the security guard's, he easily got them up on the beach. Tanner jumped out of the boat and pushed them up onto the sand while Maine sat there, his chest heaving.

"You need to eat," Orchid said, going into mother mode again. She pulled out three protein bars and held them out. "Let's each eat one of these now. There are four bottles of water in here. We should each drink one too. Then we can start looking for food and making more water."

She had a desalination kit in her pack, as well as emergency blankets, vitamins, a knife, cord, and several other packages of food. Eden had made sure she'd have what she'd need in case of emergency, and she could hear her younger sister saying, "You won't need it, Orchid. But just in case."

Just in case had arrived. Orchid did need every single thing in this pack, and she didn't let Maine take it before she stepped out of the boat. He and Tanner had refused the food earlier, but they didn't now. Each of them took the protein bar and bottle of water from her.

With things distributed, she wrapped her arms around Maine and held on tight. "We made it," he whispered into her hair, and Orchid wondered what the fluttery feeling in her lungs meant.

"We made it dry land," she said, facing the forest up the beach a ways. "Now we have to figure out how to survive here until someone finds us." She didn't want to think about how Iris and Justin had waited, eating only dragon fruit and rambutans, only to realize no one would ever find them.

But you're not as far from civilization, Orchid reasoned within her own mind. Two boats had known where they were, and they still had plenty of summer daylight left to make shelter, which meant they hadn't been out on the open water for long.

She adjusted the hat she'd found in her pack and put on hours ago and started marching up the beach. "Shelter first," she said, glad when neither Maine nor Tanner argued with her.

A strange sound met her ears as she approached the tree line. "Is that…?" She didn't know how to finish, because the warbling was so odd, she couldn't quite give it a name.

"Sounds like clucking," Maine said, joining her in the shade. "Like chickens."

"There can't be chickens out here," Orchid said, though now that he'd said that, the sound definitely seemed chicken-like.

"Do you know how to build a shelter?" Maine asked out of the corner of his mouth as a huffing and puffing Tanner came up behind them.

"No clue," Orchid said under her breath, hoping Maine hadn't heard her. She turned to Tanner. "He's kind of deaf, so what do you think that sounds like?"

He cocked his head, the dark hair falling into his eyes. "Sounds like chickens."

Orchid almost scowled. "It can't be chickens." Just as she finished, a chicken strutted right in front of them. Orchid stared at it, and then looked at Maine.

"It's a chicken," they said together, and Orchid's mouth actually started to water.

Maine whooped and laughed, sweeping Orchid right off her feet as he spun around. Sand sprayed out, and the warbling chicken squawked. Orchid couldn't help laughing, though she knew that bird wouldn't be making itself into chicken noodle soup.

Maine set her down and gazed at her. Something hot and instant sparked between them, and Orchid only had a moment to wonder what in the world was happening before Tanner said, "Uh, guys. You better get up here. You're not going to believe this."

CHAPTER SIX

*M*aine looked at Orchid, and as one unit, they started into the trees. He'd been hesitating, because the chicken had freaked him out a little. A chicken. Maine wasn't afraid of three-hundred-pound linebackers, but a five-pound chicken had given him anxiety.

He needed to pull himself together. Get his head in the game.

The air cooled out of the sun, and he jogged over to where Tanner stood, gazing at something. Maine could tell there was something not quite right about this area, but he couldn't put his finger on exactly what it was.

Until he stood next to Tanner and realized he was looking at a house. Or what used to be a house. A crude treehouse. But still. A house. On this deserted island.

"There have been people here before," he said as Orchid arrived, somewhat out of breath. He continued to scan the area, and there were supplies here. A bucket. Rudimentary tools.

"Holy crap," Orchid said, and that launched Maine into motion again. He strode forward and started picking through the things lying on a flat surface that may have been a table years ago. Many years ago.

It didn't matter. There was wood here. The bucket didn't fall apart when he picked it up. The spear fit in his hand just fine. A sense of wonder filled him, and he turned back to find the others had spread out and were examining things too.

"This is incredible," Orchid called. "There's a boat over here. It's damaged, but it's definitely a boat."

Maine left the trinkets on the table and went to look at the boat. He'd just arrived when more squabbles filled the air. "I can't believe there are chickens here," he said, looking around for them. But the lower vegetation kept them hidden. "How do you think they got here?"

"I think this is one of the islands they used in World War Two," Orchid said. "Remember how the United States had coast watchers on islands?"

Maine did not remember that. He had no idea that had happened, but he'd been more focused on sports than academics throughout his life. "Fascinating," he said.

A new sound filled the air, and Maine cocked his head, not trusting his faulty ears. "Do you hear that?"

"I'm not deaf," Orchid said. As soon as she said it, she sucked in a breath. "I mean, I'm sorry, Maine." She threaded her fingers through his, and he squeezed her hand.

"It's fine," he said, smiling at her. "Honestly, I know I can't hear."

"You obviously can."

"It's hard when there's a lot going on," he said. "Music, chatter, noise." He needed her to understand. "I swear I didn't hear you say your name the first time we met."

She blinked, those tropical eyes so mesmerizing. "You heard Amber."

"Amber?"

"She waltzed up and said her name, and you said yours." She ducked her head and toed the sand. "I got upset and stomped away."

"I saw that," he said. "I wasn't sure what had happened. "I don't remember hearing Amber. I think I saw her mouth move, so I assumed she'd said her name."

Orchid looked at him again, and the whole world stopped spinning. He'd never felt like this before, at least not with a woman. Several times during games, time would slow and stop as the football flew through the air. Every breath in the stadium held while they all waited to see if the receiver would catch the ball or not.

"I hate to say it," she said, her voice playful and flirty. "But you should probably get hearing aids." She shrugged one shoulder like she didn't care, added a laugh to the statement, and said, "I think that sounds like a pig."

Maine turned as the sound got louder, and sure enough a wild boar came crashing through the undergrowth a moment later. He yelped, pushed Orchid behind him, and wished he hadn't left the spear over by the tree.

"Holy mother of pearl," he said, his heart hammering. "What do we do?"

"I'm not trained in how to deal with wild animals," Orchid said, both of her hands clutching his forearm as she peeked around him.

The pig stood there and stared at Maine, his eyes a little beady and definitely wild. "No wonder the house is in the tree," he said, refusing to check to see where Tanner had gone. Part of him wanted to be alone on this island with Orchid, and the other part of him was glad he had more help. Because he was so far out of his element, he wasn't even sure he could survive the night.

A thunderous cracking sound filled the air, and Maine looked to the tree house to find Tanner yelling as he fell right through the floor of it.

"So much for that," Orchid said, and Maine's heartbeat crackled like the broken wood. Where would they sleep now? No way he could lie down on the sand and hope a chicken didn't peck his eyes out while he slept.

No freaking way.

The pig darted into the foliage, and Maine started for the tree house. One, he needed to make sure Tanner was okay, and two, he felt safer where other humans had once lived.

"You okay, man?" he asked, extending his hand for Tanner to take. The other man lay partially on his side, his breathing coming quicker and quicker.

"He's not okay," Orchid said, kneeling beside him. "Tanner. Look at me."

He did, thankfully, but the pain was etched all over his face.

"What hurts?" she demanded, her hands hovering above him. Maine couldn't see any blood. His legs weren't twisted underneath him. But Maine also knew that some injuries weren't obvious to others—like his hearing loss.

"My back," Tanner ground out between clenched teeth. "I had surgery on it eight weeks ago."

"And you were working?" Orchid moved around to his back.

"I stood on a ship," Tanner said, agony in every word. "I was fine."

"Yes, well, you're not fine now." Orchid looked up at Maine, clear questions in her eyes. But Maine had no idea what to do to help Tanner. He'd seen plenty of guys get hurt and get taken off the field. The trainers and physicians wouldn't let them move. They fed them painkillers and took x-rays and body scans and made statements to the press.

"He needs to remain immobile," Maine said, crouching down. "There's a table over here. We could use it like a stretcher." He met Tanner's eyes. "Okay, bro? Let's get you on that, and then we'll see what else we can do."

"I have painkillers," Orchid said, jumping ot her feet and rushing over to her backpack. Maine turned and cleared the rudimentary spoons and bowls and the bucket off the table. He dragged it over to Tanner and placed it behind his back.

"Can you lay flat?" he asked, putting one hand on Tanner's shoulder.

"Let's try it," he said, groaning as he rolled. Maine helped by pushing down his shoulder and shifting the table underneath him so he was all the way on it.

Tanner yelled, and Maine froze. Orchid had too, fear marching across her face. She shook it off and came over with a fist full of pills. "Take these," she said, though Tanner was clearly in no shape to take the meds. He panted, and sweat had broken out along his forehead.

"Tanner," she said in a stern voice. "Take these."

He opened his mouth, and she poured the pills in. "Water," she said, and Maine scrambled to find the bottle he'd been drinking from. It was with the discarded utensils, and he returned to find Tanner had swallowed them dry.

Orchid set to work plucking leaves from the banyan trees, and she returned to Tanner and placed them under his head. "You'll be okay," she said. "I know help is already coming."

"Thank you," he whispered, his eyes closed. "Don't let me sleep too long, okay?"

Maine wasn't sure they should let him fall asleep at all, but Orchid ran her fingers across his forehead and pushed his hair back in such a tender, maternal way that Maine didn't say anything.

She met his eye, and she pulled away from Tanner quickly. Maine stared at her, sure there was more to her than she'd let on. "Are you a nurse?" he asked.

"No," she said.

"What do you do for a living?"

"I'm an administrative assistant for a flower company." She wouldn't look at him, and Maine didn't like that. Not one little bit.

She walked over to the tools and surveyed them. "Bowls, spoons, a bucket." She stacked everything in the bucket and picked it up.

"There's a spear too," he said, finding it closer to the tree trunk. He glanced up. "I was really hoping to sleep up there tonight."

"We need shelter and water," she said. "We can live on another couple of meals of protein bars until we figure out food."

"There are chickens and pigs," Maine said quietly. "They're food."

"Food that requires fire," Orchid said.

"There's plenty of wood here."

"True," she said. "Should we start with shelter?" She glanced over her shoulder to Tanner, and Maine did too. His chest rose and fell in an even pattern, and he hoped he wasn't in too much pain.

"I'm going to check out the tree house," he said, putting down the spear. "Just see how big it is. Maybe there's part of it we can use."

"We'll never get Tanner into it," she said. "He's huge."

Maine agreed, but he said nothing as he started up the decades-old ladder that had been nailed into the trunk. He poked his head through the opening to see the tree house was much bigger than he'd thought. Tanner had fallen through a section on the edge to his right, but there was still plenty of space up here.

"Come up," he said to Orchid as he pulled himself up the last couple of feet and into the structure.

He tested his weight with each step, not wanting to fall the fifteen feet to the ground the way Tanner had. No, he hadn't just had back surgery, but he could twist an ankle or break a leg, and that would be catastrophic for his career.

Just being out here was catastrophic for his career.

Frustration boiled through him, but he navigated the entire left side of the tree house without any problems. He could easily lie down up here, and so could Orchid. If they could get Tanner up here, he could too.

"Plenty of room," he said when Orchid's blonde head popped up.

"Is it safe?"

Structurally, yes, Maine thought so. But having her so close to him was definitely going to be oh-so-dangerous to his health. His heart seemed to do flips in his chest as she continued up and started gingerly placing her feet on the boards, the same way he had.

"What do you think?" he asked.

"I think it'll be better than sleeping in sand," she said.

Maine chuckled, glad when Orchid came to stand next to him. He didn't dare go all the way over to the edge but stayed more toward the middle. He could still see out into the trees, and when he looked over his shoulder, he felt like he could see way out across the ocean.

He sighed as he lifted his arm and put it around Orchid. "So," he said, unsure if he should venture into these waters. But he had to know. "You've been married before?"

She flinched but didn't look at him. "Yes. How did you know?"

He wrestled with what to tell her. "You said something about your husband's boat going under," he finally said. "Back on the ship."

"I don't remember that."

She'd been freaking out, but Maine didn't need to point that out. "You don't have to tell me if you don't want to," he said, kneading her shoulder closer. "But I think it's pretty clear...." He let his voice trail into silence, because he was suddenly unsure what was so clear.

"What?" she asked, tipping her head back to look at him.

Gazing into those eyes, he found the courage he needed. "I like you," he said. "I think we would've had a great cruise together, and I would've asked you out once we got back to land."

A smile slowly spread her lips. "You think so?"

The powerful electricity crackling through him testified of it. "Yeah," he simply said. He wanted to ask her if she could feel that charge between them, but he didn't.

"Okay," she said, snuggling into his chest. "I would've said yes. Probably. Maybe."

"Maybe?" Maine wanted her to look at him again, but she steadfastly kept her eyes out on the water. "You were on a singles cruise, Orchid. What was your goal?"

She didn't answer, and Maine had just about given up hope that she would when she said, "I didn't really have one."

CHAPTER SEVEN

Orchid couldn't seem to find the right words to tell Maine about Henry. And not only him, Tesla too.

"My boss said I had to take some time off." She forced a laugh out of her too-tight throat. "It's a funny story, actually. His father bought some gifts for a few of us at the company, but he didn't realize the cruises were for StarMatch. My sister booked it before I could stop her, because she thinks it's time for me to move on."

Maine said nothing. Just stood a half-step behind her, his body warm and comforting.

"So I didn't really have a goal," she said. "I tried to mingle and go to the activities so I could tell Ivy I did. I was honestly expecting the whole thing to be miserable, and a big flop."

"Well, it's sort of that," he said, his breath tickling

her earlobe. "I mean, this island isn't going to be a barrel of fun."

Orchid knew that, and she nodded, glad when Maine's other arm came around her as she shifted to stand more in front of him. Half of her cells were self-conscious, screaming at her to move away from him before he felt how many extra pounds she carried. The other half of her body wanted to stay right where it was, enjoy the prickling, tickling sensations of the sparks running along her skin.

She hadn't felt this way for so long. Too long.

"I was married a long time ago," she said. "His name was Henry. We were only married for eighteen months before his yacht sunk. He was lost at sea. I buried an empty coffin." Orchid was aware her voice had dropped, and she hoped Maine had heard her. She didn't want to repeat it.

"That's terrible," he said. "I'm so sorry."

And that wasn't even the worst of it. She scrambled for the right words, and they simply didn't seem to be there. "I had our baby six months later."

Behind her, Maine tensed instantly. "You're kidding."

"I'm not," she said. "I have a seven-year-old daughter name Tesla." Desperation clogged her throat. "I have to get off this island, Maine. My child will not be an orphan." She spoke with absolute conviction.

"We'll get out of here," he promised, and Orchid liked the idea of relying on him. She'd only had herself for so long, and she'd failed so many times. Her family had been a great support to her, and she twisted into Maine's full embrace.

"Tell me about your family," she said. He'd kept her babbling about her sisters and their ordeals on the cliffs and off the coast of Maui for the boat ride here.

"I have two sisters," he said. "One older, one younger. Honey and Diana." He sounded a bit robotic, and Orchid pulled away and stepped back toward the tree trunk. She was aware Maine had not gotten too close to the edge of the tree house, where the railing was. He was cautious, and she had not expected that from the football celebrity.

"You're freaked out about my daughter," she said, taking in his face in one sweeping look.

"No," he said, and he wasn't a great liar either.

"It's okay," she said, though it stung a little bit, right behind her lungs. "I know it's a lot to take in all at once."

Maine searched her face, the seconds piling on top of one another. "I have a five-year-old nephew," he said. "Kids don't scare me."

"Have you ever dated a woman with children?" She didn't mean to sound so challenging.

"No," he admitted.

"Do you want kids?"

"I mean, sure." He shrugged. "I haven't thought about it all that much, to be honest."

"Focused on your career." Orchid knew the type,

and she turned away from him. "We need to get our water situation figured out."

"Orchid," he said, touching her upper arm. The skin there burned, but she didn't pull away. He sighed like she was being difficult on purpose. She wasn't, but she didn't know how to flirt like Ivy. She didn't have a carefree life. She had a job and a child and responsibilities.

And fear. So much fear.

"I *have* been focused on my career," he said. "But recently, I've really wanted to find someone to spend my life with." A hint of redness crept into his face. "For the last couple of years, I've tried, and every relationship has been a disaster."

She wondered what his definition of disaster was, but she didn't ask. "I haven't dated in eight years, since my husband died."

Maine looked like he'd been hit with a cruise ship, and Orchid turned away from him again. "I'll be right back."

"Orchid," he said again, but she found her footing on the rungs and went down to the ground. He didn't follow her and didn't call her back again. It was okay. He needed some time to absorb everything she'd said.

Heck, had she been in his position, she would need some time and space to think through things. "He thought you were a fun, flirty, single woman," she muttered to herself. Well, maybe not fun or flirty. And she *was* single.

But single with a lot of baggage.

Though, he seemed to have some of his own, too, and Orchid actually liked that. Maine Fitzgerald seemed so unstoppable on the football field. He was one hundred yards of pure muscle and power, and he never looked ruffled or frustrated during a game. Never.

Orchid walked away from the tree house, reminding herself of the wild animals on this island. She couldn't go too far, but she ventured back to the boat, deciding to fill it with banyan leaves and palm fronds so they'd have something besides bare wood to sleep on in just a few hours.

Her back hurt too, though she knew it wasn't even close to the pain Tanner had to be experiencing. She was simply out of shape, and sitting in a boat and then walking through sand and climbing ladders didn't make her soggy muscles very happy.

But she stretched and picked, bent and gathered, until she had a good pile of leaves and fronds. She'd piled them all in the boat, and she walked around to the back of it to try pushing it.

Something sharp touched her foot. She jerked away, as the last thing she needed was an injury. A seashell glinted there, a ray of sunlight falling through the trees to highlight it. Thinking only of her daughter, Orchid bent to pick up the shell. It was white on one side, with a pale pink interior.

Tesla would love this shell, though she had hundreds of them from her time snorkeling at Shell Reef, the best place in Hawaii to find shells. This one was mostly intact, while many of Tesla's weren't. The tides and waves that came ashore didn't play nicely with seashells, as she'd told her daughter numerous times.

She tucked this shell in the pocket of her shorts and turned to heave her weight into the boat. It only moved a few feet, but it was enough to get what little strength she possessed behind it and keep it moving across the sand.

Tanner tossed his head and groaned, and Orchid wanted to get him up into the shelter before darkness fell.

Exhaustion hit her, and she stopped pushing the boat. There was so much to do, and so little time to do it in.

Maine approached from the other direction, a bunch of bananas in his hand. "Orchid," he said, his eyes all lit up. "I found a garden. Come see."

She immediately started toward him, taking a banana when he handed it to her. The fruit tasted like manna from heaven, and she smiled at him. She didn't feel the need to explain any more to him, and the ball was in his court now.

Or his yard line. Whatever. She'd told him about her husband and daughter, and he could decide what to do with that information.

"The pigs have obviously found it too," he said. "But there's still some really good stuff." He marched along a path that had probably been well-worn in the past but now had grasses and bushes trying to eradicate it from the earth.

She followed him, buoyed by his excitement. "How far is it?" she asked, glancing left and then right. The water still washed ashore on her right, so they were walking parallel to the ocean.

"Just back here," he said, taking a right when she expected him to go left. They moved back out in to the sun, and sure enough, a garden spread before her. Well, an overrun garden, full of weeds and plants that should've been pruned back long ago.

It didn't matter. It was food, and delight filled her. She started laughing as she moved into the mess of greenery. Maine joined her, his deeper chuckles making harmony with her higher laughter.

He bent and pulled something up, a long, orange carrot now in his hand. "Look." He smiled at the carrot as if he'd never seen one before. Orchid felt the same way, a sense of wonder and happiness filling her in a place where she'd expected to be frightened and miserable.

"Let's take a bunch of stuff back," she said. "Put it in the tree house. Figure out how to get Tanner up there. And desalinate some water for morning." She looked at him. "Yeah?"

"Yeah," he said. "And I'll figure out how to keep the pigs out of the garden. This place is amazing."

Orchid bent again, her back protesting, and started picking plants. Half of them came out with nothing attached but a root. A weed. But she found carrots and potatoes and even a beet. One single beet.

"How do you think they planted this stuff?" she asked.

"They had to bring it with them," he said. "I mean, they had to have tools to build that tree house. The table. All of it."

"Do you think they left any behind?"

"I don't know," he said, glancing up as the light started to fade. Panic hit Orchid right in the chest. "I can go exploring in the morning."

"We should get back," she said, forming a carrying pouch with her T-shirt.

Maine nodded and pulled his shirt over his head. He started piling the vegetables he'd found on it, but all Orchid could do was stare at his bare torso. He was tan and glorious, with ridged muscles as far as the eye could see.

Everything inside her heated, and she tore her eyes away and started back to the tree house. Maine came behind her a few seconds later, and she felt every inch of her skin during the walk back.

"Leaves," he said. "Great idea." He beamed at her and went up the ladder with his food.

"Toss your shirt down," she said. "I'll put my veggies in it and pass it up to you."

He did as she suggested, and she stepped up a couple of rungs until he could get his hands on the fabric of his shirt. Then she started passing leaves up to him too, until the entire boat full was in the tree house.

"I'm going to fill up the water bottles," she said, collecting the empty one beside Tanner. "Where's yours?"

"That one's mine," he said, nodding over the edge of the tree house. So he was being a little braver now. "I don't know where Tanner's is."

Orchid frowned. They only had four bottles, and now one was missing. She shook the negativity away. She couldn't afford to go into one of her depressive slumps out here. She had to get back to Tesla.

She had to stay busy. Keep her mind off how weak and pathetic she was. Turning, she grabbed the bucket with the bowls and piled the two water bottles in with them. The sand was hot on the way to the water, but Orchid ignored the flames in her feet.

After filling everything she could with the cleanest water possible, she lugged it all back up the beach. Her heart pounded and her shoulders wailed at her to *stop with all the working*.

She didn't stop. She kept one eye on Tanner, her mind riddling through what they were going to do with him, while she pulled the desalination tablets from her backpack. She read the instructions, noting that the big, bold letters said EMERGENCY USE ONLY.

Well, this was an emergency. She put the tablets in the water and watched them. She wasn't sure what she expected. Bubbling, maybe. Something. Nothing happened at all. Her hopes deflated quickly, and she couldn't push against the rising tide of desperation.

In that moment, her eyes also caught on something else on the package. These were water purification tablets, not water desalination tablets. They wouldn't take the salt out of the ocean water.

She fell back, utterly exhausted now. She hadn't even realized she'd started weeping until Maine said, "Hey, hey, hey. What's wrong?" He enveloped her in his strong arms, and Orchid hated that she needed that. Needed him.

"Nothing." She sat up and pushed him away. "But this water isn't drinkable. These aren't desalination tablets."

He looked at her blankly, and Orchid wanted to rage at him, though she wasn't any smarter than him. "There has to be a way to get drinking water," she said. She grabbed her pack. "Surely Eden would've made sure I could get drinking water."

She started pulling things out of the pack and naming them. "Emergency blankets. Unbreakable cord. All-in-one tool. Can cooker. Nail clippers. First aid kit. Painkillers. Antibiotics. Plastic gloves. Tarp. Hey." She looked up at Maine, who also wore a grim expression despite the hope shining in those dark blue eyes. "We could've used this to carry the vegetables."

"We will tomorrow," he said. "There are fruit trees here too. Loads of them." He nodded back to her backpack. "Anything else?"

She pulled out a mess kit, a flashlight with fresh batteries, and a fire-starting kit. "And this." She put the box on the sand between them. "A solar still." The picture on the box looked like a floating balloon on water, and she clapped her hands.

"This is it. This is a solar kit to evaporate water and make it drinkable." The bright red letters in the corner confirmed it, and her hands tripped over themselves to get the device out.

"The sun's going down," Maine said. "We should wait until morning."

Orchid was suddenly so thirsty. She didn't want to wait until morning, but she didn't want their only way to make the miles and miles of water surrounding them to float away in the darkness either.

"Orchid?" he asked. "Okay? I'll take care of this in the morning."

"Okay." She nodded, biting the inside of her cheek to keep herself from crying. "I'll get rid of all this water." She stood up, but Maine took her into his arms before she could move.

"Leave it," he whispered. "I'll take care of it too. Okay? Let's figure out how to get Tanner into the tree house, and then it's time for bed." He rubbed her back, and Orchid enjoyed the warmth from his body, the safety in his arms, despite the despair she felt clawing at her.

CHAPTER EIGHT

*M*aine stayed still, his hands having a mind of their own as they continued to stroke Orchid's back. She held him tight, like she needed him, and Maine wanted to be the man for her. The one who cradled her while she cried, and took care of her, and made sure she never experienced unhappiness again.

The feelings were strange and new for him, and he absolutely welcomed them. It was nice to think about someone else for a change, and feel like perhaps his only worth didn't depend on how far and how accurate he could throw a ball.

He finally swept his lips along her cheek. Then her earlobe, his pulse quickening when she leaned into his touch. He pressed his mouth to her temple and whispered, "Come on."

She stepped out of his arms and looked at Tanner,

who was still asleep on the tabletop. Maine knelt down and shook his shoulder. "Tanner," he said, his quarterback bark coming out of his mouth. "Wake up. We need you to climb into the tree house."

The man's eyelids fluttered and opened, and he blinked as awareness came over him.

"Can you get up?" Maine asked. "We don't want you to sleep on the sand." He didn't really want Tanner in the tree house either, because then he couldn't whisper with Orchid, tell her how wonderful and beautiful she was, and kiss her until she moaned his name.

He buried the fantasies as Tanner eased himself to a sitting position. "Yeah, I can get up."

Maine looked at Orchid. "All right. Slowly, now." He braced himself and extended his hand to Tanner, who took it and leaned his whole weight against Maine's to get to his feet. He groaned as pain flashed through his dark eyes.

"We're going back up there?" he asked, holding very still.

"It's okay on the left side," Maine said. "I've been up there a lot." He'd stood at the railing and watched Orchid walk down to the water's edge and fill up the containers. He'd almost felt removed from her, from the whole world, in that moment, and he didn't hate it. He'd lived a life of football, and he was starting to think there was more for him out there.

Like a pretty blonde and her daughter.

"One step at a time," Maine said. "Orchid, will you go up first in case he needs help at the top?"

She shouldered her pack, scampered in front of them, and scaled the rungs easily. "See?" he said to Tanner. "Easy." But he knew sometimes with a back injury, lifting a leg was in fact very difficult.

Tanner did it, hoisting his weight up onto the first rung. Step by step, he got himself into the tree house. Maine glanced around at the sandy ground, the water bowls and bucket near the trunk, and reached for the spear. Might as well be prepared.

He climbed into the tree house too, hoping the job he'd done with the leaves and fronds would meet Orchid's approval. She hovered over Tanner, who lay with his back right against the outer wall of the structure.

A blip of unease ran through Maine, and he stepped past them to the back of the tree house, hoping to distribute their weight more evenly. He'd piled the leaves for pillows, and he sank down near the one he wanted.

Orchid came over a few seconds later and curled right into his chest as easily as if she'd done it thousands of times before. "I'm so tired," she murmured.

"Me too," Maine said, taking in a long, deep breath of her hair. "We'll find water in the morning, Orchid. Think about it. There are chickens and pigs here. They can't drink ocean water either."

She stiffened in his arms. "You're right," she said, a new edge of happiness in her voice. "You're so right."

He lay still as she shifted and relaxed into his embrace again. "The stars will be beautiful out here," he whispered.

"I've got my eyes closed already," Orchid said back, her breath brushing the collar of his shirt.

"I'll describe them to you," he said, the darkness becoming deeper and deeper with each breath he took. But he said nothing. Just watched as the pinpricks of light appeared in the little of the sky he could see through the canopy of the tree above him.

Eventually, his eyelids drifted closed and he entered the peaceful bliss of slumber.

HE WOKE TO THE SOUND OF A ROOSTER crowing, and it was akin to torture. If he knew what torture was—and right now, it was the obnoxious wail of a chicken before the sun had even risen.

Orchid groaned in his arms, and Maine knew exactly how she felt. His bones and muscles felt rusty, and he wondered what time it was.

"That's the first one I'm going to kill," he said, even his throat full of frogs this morning.

Orchid giggled, which sent Maine to laughing too. He had a ton of work to do that day, but for right now, he just wanted to laugh with this gorgeous, strong woman. He quieted a few seconds before Orchid did, and he opened his eyes to look at her.

She still had her eyes closed, the crinkly lines of laughter around them as she continued to smile. He wondered what she'd do if he kissed her right now. Right this second. His heartbeat picked up as he seized hold of the thought. He cradled her face in both hands, pushing her hair back a split second before he lowered his mouth to hers.

Orchid flinched and pulled back, giving Maine the answer to his question. "Sorry," he whispered, opening his eyes again. She looked into his, and he had no idea what to say next. He knew her rejection stung, and he knew he just wanted to go back to sleep. Maybe when he woke up, this will all have been a nightmare, and he'll go to the snack bar and get one of those virgin drinks he liked so much.

"It's okay," Orchid whispered, pressing in closer to him. Her eyelids drifted closed again, and she tilted her head toward his, almost begging him to kiss her.

He didn't want to take her by surprise again, and he honestly wasn't sure what she was telling him. Any other woman, and he'd know. But Orchid was complicated. She felt things deeply, and she wasn't afraid to show her emotions. Maine found her refreshing and puzzling at the same time.

"Are you going to kiss me?" she murmured, the words barely registering in Maine's ears.

"Do you want me to?"

She snuggled closer, if that were possible. "Yes."

"I just thought—I mean, you—"

"Don't think so much." She leaned into him and kissed him then, and Maine's head filled with heat, driving all his thoughts away. He accelerated the kiss, almost showing her how hungry he was for this type of human connection, and then pulled back slowly, making every stroke gentle and slow.

Her fingers slid through his hair, sending showers of electricity down his shoulders and back. "Orchid," he whispered, removing his lips from hers for the two-syllable word and kissing her neck next.

The adrenaline pumping through him felt the same as when he threw a game-winning touchdown. He didn't think such a thing was possible, but this woman was full of surprises. He wanted to know every one of them, and he moved his mouth back to hers.

Finally, he pulled away, enjoying being kissed and kissing her a whole lot. "I should go take care of the water," he whispered. "You stay here and go back to sleep. I'll be right back." He eased away from her, his eyes able to see well enough in the pre-dawn grayness surrounding them.

He went down the ladder and stooped to empty the bowls and bucket of the sea water she'd gathered last night. He set them on the tabletop before he remembered she had the solar desalination system in her backpack.

He turned to find her coming down the ladder, her

backpack clutched in one hand. He took it from her before she fell. "You didn't have to get up," he said.

"I'm not going to go back to sleep," she said, barely meeting his eye. She took in the bucket and bowls and said, "Let's go get fruit and veggies." She bent and extracted the tarp from her backpack. "And we can explore before it gets too hot."

"We can't do the water until the sun's up anyway."

"Right." She finally looked at him, and Maine grinned at her, completely unembarrassed about the kiss in the tree house.

"So that." He cleared his throat. "That was okay?"

"That, meaning you kissed me?"

"I think *you* kissed *me*," he said, a smile shining through his whole soul now.

Orchid's blue eyes seemed full of fire as she finally smiled too. "Yeah, that was okay."

"Just okay?" he asked, a bit self-conscious. "I maybe haven't kissed a woman in a while."

She stepped up to him, balanced on her toes, and held onto his shoulders. "It was great, Maine." She kissed him again, and he vowed the next time they kissed, he was going to initiate it. "Now, let's go make sure we don't die today. I have a daughter to get home to."

She picked up the backpack while Maine grabbed the tarp. "Tell me about her," he said as they set out. "Your daughter."

"She loves to paint and draw," Orchid said, her

voice a little tense. But Maine wasn't sure, as the grasses were rustling with their footsteps, and Orchid was in front of him. "She loves going on grandpa dates with my dad and Henry's dad. She loves the beach and seashells."

"My nephew is into creepy crawly things," Maine said. "Spiders, snakes, bugs. My sister says it drives her nuts."

Orchid laughed. "I bet it does. Tesla wants a puppy, but we're not home enough."

Maine wanted her to be able to stay home, do whatever she wanted. He'd buy them both a dog and wave to them on camera when he traveled for games. He kept all these thoughts inside, and as they reached the garden, he said, "Favorite game. I'll go first. Favorite food: bacon cheeseburger."

Orchid looked at him, her eyes wide. "I don't know how to play this game."

Maine got to work spreading the tarp out beside the edge of the garden. "It's easy. I started with favorite food. I named mine. Now you have to name yours. Then you pick the next favorite. Say it, and I share mine. We go until one of us names a favorite and the other one doesn't have one."

"So there's a winner."

Maine looked at her. "Not really. I mean, if you want there to be a winner." Maybe she did. From her show in the Battle of the Sexes, he'd learned she was competitive.

"I don't need there to be a winner." She bent and yanked on a fistful of leaves. "Onion rings."

"That's your favorite food?"

"Yes," she said. "Are there wrong answers?"

"No," he said with a chuckle. "I just wasn't expecting that."

"What were you expecting?"

"I don't know," he said as he started pulling up greenery in the garden. "Sushi, maybe. Or fish tacos. You grew up on the island."

"I don't even like fish."

"How very un-Hawaiian of you," he teased. "Seems like most people I've met who've lived on the island for a while are fish freaks."

"My mom would be one of them," Orchid said. "I guess salmon is all right. But I'm not crazy about fish."

"So onion rings," he said, pulling up a good haul of potatoes. He shook the dirt off and tossed them onto the tarp. "You get to name the next favorite."

"TV show," she said. "Chopped."

"I don't even know what that is," he said.

"It's a cooking show," she said. "They compete with unknown ingredients."

"Wonder how they'd do out here."

She laughed as she put two carrots on the tarp. "They'd probably all have a fire built in under five minutes."

Apprehension moved through Maine. "Do you think we need a fire?"

"No," she said.

"Maybe the smoke would help the rescue ship find us."

"Maybe." She paused and looked out toward the ocean. The water was black still, without the shining light of the sun, and Maine felt the ominous way it constantly pounded against the shore as he watched it.

"Something to think about," he said. "You had a fire-starting kit in the backpack."

"Maybe we should start a fire this afternoon," she said. "After we get food and explore the island to see if there's water. We should probably boil it before drinking it anyway."

She had a good point, and Maine felt the weight of the day ahead.

"Your turn," she said, pulling him back to this lighter moment. "Favorite TV show."

CHAPTER NINE

*O*rchid enjoyed the favorite game with Maine, as it kept her mind busy with something care-free while she worked. They pulled as many vegetables and picked as much fruit as they could carry, finally returning to the tree house and Tanner after a couple of hours.

He was awake and standing up in the shelter. He had good color, and Orchid offered him a drink from their last water bottle. He took it and said, "Thank you guys so much. I'm going to try to help today."

"Nope," Orchid said as she spread the tarp out near the back of the shelter, to the right of where she and Maine had slept the night before. The hole Tanner had made when he'd fallen through the floor was still several feet away, and everything seemed stable. "Not happening. Maine is going to set the solar filtration system as soon as we get the food up here. You can babysit that while we explore the island for a spring or a river or something."

She didn't allow a single ounce of desperation to enter her mind, though it pressed against the barrier she kept there. She had to be strong out here. Tesla needed her back in Getaway Bay, and Orchid would get back to her.

Having a dreamy man to kiss helped too, but something niggled in the back of Orchid's mind. He was a professional football player. Sure, he liked cheeseburgers and watching the sun set, but that didn't make him normal.

Or permanent, her mind whispered, playing devil's advocate to the chirpy, happy angel on the other shoulder that was just thrilled Orchid had finally branched out and gotten herself a boyfriend.

And Orchid had no plans to leave Getaway Bay or the support system she currently had. Not only that, Tesla deserved a father who was going to be in the picture more than every other weekend.

This new burden sat heavily on her shoulders, but she hadn't dared give it much room in her mind. She hadn't asked Maine about his travel schedule or his long-term plans for his career. *Maybe he's ready to retire*, she told herself, getting that devilish voice to shut up.

Maine kept passing up carrots and potatoes by the bucket full. She dumped them on the tarp and passed it back, taking the bowl he'd piled bananas into. Their system worked great, and she was glad she was in the tree house this time, instead of going up and down the ladder, even if it was only a few rungs.

Maine was taller than her, so he only had to take two steps up for her to reach the bucket, and they got the food loaded into the tree house pretty quickly.

"Tanner's going to come down," Orchid said, nodding at him. He moved like a ninety-year-old man, but he made it back to the ground.

"I'll go set this up," Maine said, jogging away with the solar desalination kit.

"You just have to watch it," Orchid said. "We don't want it to get swept away or anything."

"Do you think there's fresh water on the island somewhere?" Tanner asked, easing himself onto the overturned bucket, using it as a tiny chair for his huge frame.

"Maybe," Orchid said. "There are chickens and pigs here. They have to drink something."

He nodded, his eyebrows drawn down into a V as he watched Maine. "Where'd you get the vegetables?"

"There's a garden down the path a ways," she said. "Tons of fruit trees too."

"We should try to trap a chicken," he said.

She couldn't disagree, but she wanted water more than drumsticks. "We will, I think," she said. "Depends on how things go today."

He nodded again, and Maine finally came back up the beach, the little raft floating only a few feet out in the water. "I think I got it set up right." He turned to look at it. "Says it takes a couple of hours, depending on the heat and strength of the sun." He looked from Tanner to Orchid. "Should we go?"

She picked up her pack, which had everything in it, and tried to look braver than she felt inside. "Yep, ready."

"Do you want the spear?" Maine asked Tanner, and he nodded again. Maine went up into the tree house to get it, and then he and Orchid set off into the trees. A sense of foreboding accompanied them, and Orchid didn't like it.

"He seems okay," she said. "Quiet."

"Maybe his back hurts."

"Maybe." She kept her eyes trained on the ground so she could step without tripping. She wasn't exactly equipped with hiking boots and bug spray, and her skin prickled as the sound of clucking met her ears.

"We're close." Maine slowed, and Orchid pressed right up into him. She glanced over her shoulder. She didn't want one of the wild pigs to catch her unawares. He continued through the trees and undergrowth for several more paces, and then they emerged into a clearing.

"Uh, Orchid?" His voice sounded unsure and filled with awe at the same time.

Orchid moved the last step to stand beside him, taking in the scene before her. It legit looked like a farm from the distant past. There were fences with chicken wire and everything. Old troughs that didn't have water anymore. The ground was well-worn, without vegetation, and she couldn't count the number of chickens there were.

"There's probably fifty of them here," she said, trying to count and getting confused as the chickens moved around. They ventured out into the grass on all sides, and some sat on nests they'd built themselves.

"This is unbelievable," Maine said. "How do they survive? Surely some die. Where are they?"

Orchid didn't want to think about it. She did want a fried egg, and she wondered if the nests had unfertilized eggs or not. At this point, these wild chickens probably didn't lay eggs that didn't hatch into chicks.

She noticed that many of them were moving off to the left, and she pointed that way. "There's a pretty prominent path over there. Maybe that's where they go to get water."

Maine followed her gaze and nodded. "Let's try it."

She was on that side, so she led them out this time, sticking close to the edge of the clearing to avoid the wild birds and their droppings. The smell here wasn't something she wanted to spend a lot of time with, that was for sure.

Most of the fences had fallen over time, but some still stood. The chickens seemed to know the paths through the clearing and out into the rest of the island, and Orchid started to appreciate their warblings as they moved around, pecking at the ground every so often.

She joined the line of animals moving down the

particular path she'd seen, and from the vantage point higher up on the hill, she could see movement for dozens of yards in front of her. "It's not close," she said.

"Can't be that far," he said. "There are troughs here. A human would've had to carry the water for the chickens when they were domesticated."

He had a fair point, and Orchid edged to the side of the path, once again avoiding the chicken's messy path. They didn't seem to care if they walked through their own waste, but she did.

Only a few minutes later, a new sound entered her ears. "Maine," she said, excitement building inside her. "Do you hear that?"

"No," he said. "What is it?"

"It's water." She started forward again, the distinct sound of water falling getting louder and louder.

Finally, Maine said, "I hear it. It's a waterfall."

"Yes." Orchid nearly ran forward, toward an outcropping of rock that had lichen growing on it. She burst out of the grass to find the chickens grouped at a pool of water. Some of them waded into the water, and one or two swam around.

"I didn't know chickens could swim," Maine said, and Orchid simply started laughing.

"They can't," she said through her giggles. "They'll sink eventually. They don't have waterproof feathers like ducks."

"How do you know this stuff?" he asked, slipping his hand into hers.

"Tesla did a science unit on birds once," she said. "That was a fact she learned, and my daughter loves to talk. And talk. And share stuff." She looked up at him, and he smiled down at her.

"There's water here," he said as if she didn't know.

"I see that."

His grin grew, and he tugged her forward. They went around the pool where the chickens drank, and the waterfall came into view. It was glorious and wonderful, falling at least thirty feet from the bluffs above. The sound of it hitting the pool below was the best sound Orchid had ever heard.

Maine started laughing and he waded into the pool, moving faster than her now. He released her hand and ducked under the falling water, slicking his hair back. He opened his mouth and tipped his head back before he came out sputtering.

Smiling. Still laughing. "There's water here."

Water that could save them. Save Tanner.

Orchid took off her backpack and followed Maine into the waterfall. It was cool and refreshing, and she couldn't help laughing too. This waterfall felt like their salvation, and they hadn't even been out here that long. But it brought hope to her heart. They had much better conditions than Iris had, and her sister had survived.

Of course, Maine wasn't a Navy SEAL, but he didn't

need to be. They had water. A garden. Chickens and pigs they could try to catch and kill and eat.

Her spirits soared, and she laughed and laughed.

Maine wound his arms around her and pulled her out of the water slightly, toward the rocks behind them. "Orchid," he said, his voice bright and serious at the same time. "I can't wait to meet your daughter."

He leaned down and kissed her in a slow, passionate way that reminded Orchid of what it felt like to be adored. Cherished. Loved.

All her worries about his residency status in Getaway Bay vanished. It was just her and him, kissing under the waterfall, and it was the most wonderful thing in the world.

***

HOURS LATER, HER CLOTHES STILL WEREN'T dry. She and Maine had made a few trips back to the waterfall, taking a different path than the one they took to the chicken meadow. The path was there, obviously used in the past once they saw it. Maine had actually spotted it from the tree house, and when he pointed it out to Orchid, she began to see all kinds of paths from the shelter.

She wanted to explore them all, but water and food came first. They had plenty of both now, and she wished she could lie out in the sun and get dry. The humidity prevented that at the moment, though the sun was plenty bright and hot.

She'd suggested they start a fire, thinking it would definitely help get their clothes dry as well as bake some potatoes and beets. She and Maine had set out to gather sticks and dry grasses, but both seemed to be in short supply.

"We could burn the table," she said, looking at the slab of wood on the ground near the tree trunk.

"Yeah," Maine said, still looking around like the supplies they needed would appear. "There's stuff in the firestarting kit. I just want to make sure we have enough fuel to keep it going."

"But we don't really need to do that," Orchid said. "If it goes out, we can just light it again the next day. There are plenty of matches."

"Yeah," Maine said again, and she wondered what he was thinking.

She asked, and he met her eye. "I'm just worried about how long we'll be out here." He looked at his hands, and Orchid did too, noticing little nicks and scrapes. He obviously wasn't used to picking vegetables and fruit or hauling buckets of water back to tree houses. She certainly wasn't either, and she wanted nothing more than to lie down and take a nap.

"You don't think we'll have enough matches to keep lighting the fire each day." She wasn't asking.

"Something like that."

"Let's go pull apart the chicken fences," she said.

"Those posts were wood. That should give us enough fuel." She touched his arm and looked up at him. "At least for today. I'm tired. I want to get a fire going. Get some food cooked. And rest. We have two matches, one for today and one for tomorrow. After that, we can keep the fire going."

Her exhaustion wasn't just physical either, but mental too. Maine looked weary as well, and he finally nodded.

"Okay. Let's use the table for today. That should be enough to bake some potatoes." He glanced around again. "I just wish there was more wood here."

"There are tons of trees," she said.

"Green ones," he responded.

"Green wood makes a lot of smoke," she said. "Maybe that will help a ship find us."

He nodded again and took her into his arms. "I think we should try climbing up on those cliffs and building a fire up there."

The very idea made her want to sag to the ground and cry. "Another day," she said, thinking maybe in two or three, they'd have enough fuel for a fire here but not one on top of the bluffs—which she didn't know how to climb or how long it would take. Not to mention, they'd have to carry all the wood up there for a big bonfire.

"Another day," he agreed, and she stepped back, pulled out the fire-starting kit, and handed it to him.

She shivered as a breeze made her wet clothes cold, and Maine noticed. "You okay?"

"Fine," she said. "Did you ever play somewhere cold in your football career?"

"I've played in the NFL for nine years," he said. "Every team's stadium. So yeah. New York is cold later in the season. So is Green Bay. Denver. Pittsburgh." He shrugged. "It's not my preference, but it's usually not too terrible."

"I've seen games get canceled because of snow," she said, wondering what that felt like. "I've lived in Hawaii my whole life. Never seen snow in person."

Maine looked at her, wonder in his face. "Really? That's fascinating."

"Not all of us are world travelers," she teased.

He chuckled and went back to the instructions. "I'm not either," he said. "That's been one of the worst parts of being with the Orcas. The travel across the ocean sucks the life right out of me. Not a fan."

Orchid stayed crouched next to him as he pulled out the fire starting chips. "Do you see yourself staying with the Orcas? Or...?" She let her question hang there, because she didn't quite know how to give it a voice.

"I don't know," he said, shrugging. "I usually just go where the money is."

"I see," Orchid said, straightening. Her back hurt anyway, and she couldn't hold such a position for much longer. Her knees ached too, and her heart seemed to be skipping every other beat.

So there was no point in her perpetuating this relationship. He was just going to follow the money wherever it took him.

Tears filled her eyes as stupidity flowed through her. She wanted to say something to him. Ask him what the heck they were doing out there if he could leave in a few months. At least excuse herself.

She said nothing as she walked away.

"Orchid," he called after her, but she just kept going.

CHAPTER TEN

*M*aine watched Orchid walk away from him, his heart sinking all the way to the ground. "Idiot," he said to himself, torn between running after her and starting the fire. He knew she wanted to dry off. She wanted to eat. He wanted both of those things too.

And maybe, just maybe, he'd been fantasizing about holding her by the fire as the stars came out tonight. Whispering his dreams of owning an ice cream shop with football-themed flavors to her. Finding out more about her and her daughter.

But now, he'd told her he just went wherever the money was. As if he needed money. He didn't. Not really.

So what do you need? he asked himself as Orchid's blonde head disappeared along the horizon. He worried about her, because she went through periods of instability. But she was strong and capable, and she had good ideas. She'd be okay out on the island, and he turned his attention back to the fire.

He had no idea what he needed. As he stacked the chips and stuffed tinder underneath them, he knew what he wanted.

Something meaningful to fill his time with. Football had always done that, because it gave him human inter-action and provided him with a way of making a living. But he couldn't cuddle with his teammates or the pigskin, and he really wanted someone to share his life with.

He wanted the orca-shaped fudge pieces in peanut butter ice cream. He wanted a family.

After striking the match, he held it to the fuzzy tinder, which caught the flame instantly. The fire chips started to blaze as well, and Maine turned to get the bigger pieces of wood. He broke apart the table and fed pieces to the growing blaze, soon having a cracking fire with smoke lifting into the air at the edge of the beach.

Pride filled him, and he really wished Orchid was there to share this victory with. He turned back to the tree house, where Tanner had gone hours ago. He climbed up the ladder quickly to find the other man asleep, his skin a bit waxy.

"Tanner," he said, alarm filling him. "Hey, man. Are you okay?" He moved over to him as the other man opened his eyes. "Come down to the beach for a bit."

Tanner let Maine help him up, and he got him

resting against the tree trunk, the fire several feet away. He dashed back up to the tree house to get a few potatoes and beets to toss into the fire.

He nestled them near the edges, having no idea how to cook in a fire pit and hoping for the best. He turned back to Tanner. "I'm going to go find Orchid, okay? If it starts to burn too low, toss another piece of wood on it." He indicated the pile he'd put next to Tanner.

"Okay," Tanner said, but he still sounded half-asleep.

"We'll eat when I get back." Maine stooped to pick up the backpack, surprised Orchid had left it behind, and started walking in the same direction she'd gone. Hopefully, she hadn't decided to circumnavigate the island or anything crazy like that.

"Orchid?" he called once he'd passed the garden. He'd never been past that on this side of their camp before, and somehow the trees and paths and beach over here looked foreign. She didn't answer, so he kept going, hoping he could hear her if she did call out to him.

He didn't go much farther before he caught sight of movement up ahead. He paused for a moment, squinting into the sunlight, before he realized it was Orchid and not a wild pig. She kept reaching up into the branches of a tree, and he recognized the movement as picking something.

"Orchid," he called again, and she turned toward

him. She didn't smile, but he pressed on toward her, finally arriving at the almond tree.

"Almonds." She acted like he'd said nothing idiotic, but he knew he had. He also didn't know how to bridge this new gap between them.

"You left the backpack," he said, setting it down.

She didn't respond, and he realized she was just dropping the nuts on the ground. He quickly swept his shirt off and started picking them up, using his clothes as a hammock to carry the food in.

"Look," he said, keeping his eyes on the sand. His fingers hurt. His head hurt. Everything hurt. "I know I sounded like a fool back there."

"I just don't see the point of us...yeah. I don't see the point of us. So let's just keep each other alive until help arrives. Then you can go back to your life, and I'll go back to mine."

Maine stood up, a raging river flowing through him now. "That's unfair."

"It is?" She faced him, her own anger evident as it washed across her face. "I'll tell you what's unfair. You acting like you like me. Kissing me under that waterfall. Making me believe that we could have something when we got back to Getaway Bay. I have a daughter, Maine. That's what's unfair." Her eyes shone like glass, but not a single tear fell.

"I didn't lead you on," he said, his fingers clenching around an almond.

She laughed, but it was full of bitterness. "Well,

you're not going to be following the money in Getaway Bay. Not forever." She went back to plucking almonds, but it was more brutal now.

"Maybe I don't want to play football anymore. Have you ever thought of that?"

"Why would I think that?" she asked. "You didn't say that. You're only thirty-one. You're the starting quarterback for the Orcas. Your whole future is in front of you. Why would I even think of that?" She faced him again, her blue eyes shooting fire at him. "I only know what you tell me."

"I'm telling you now," he said, swallowing. "And I've never told anyone this before. So maybe it's hard for me. Maybe we're not all great at saying what we feel."

"I'm not great at that either," she said. "You're the first man I've been remotely interested in, and it's just...not fair." She shook her head and looked away, some of her anger fleeing as she did.

"Hey." Maine stepped around her and made her look at him. "Hey, I'm not leaving right now."

"I'm not bringing you into my life—into my daughter's life—only to have you leave next spring when you get traded to the Pirates."

"Ew," he said. "I would never go play for the Pirates."

"You would if they paid you thirty million dollars." She glared up at him. "Tell me you wouldn't."

Maine sighed. "Maybe I would have before I met

you," he said quickly. "But Orchid...." A storm surged through him. "I *really* like you. I'm not playing games with you. And I want to meet your daughter and see if she'll like me too. And I want to open an ice cream shop that sells football-themed flavors."

He sucked in a breath, feeling weak and strong all at the same time.

Orchid searched his face. "What?"

Maine dropped to the ground again, picking up almonds like his life depended on it. "You heard me." He filled his shirt while she stood there, the weight of her eyes on the back of his head.

He finally stood, all the nuts securely tucked into his T-shirt. "I'm headed back. There's a fire going, and I put in some food to cook." He walked away, because she still hadn't said anything, and he'd never told anyone about his ice cream dream.

A pipe dream, he told himself, though he had a notebook full of ideas for flavors. He hadn't tried any recipes yet, nor did he have any idea for a name of the place, or where it would be. Nothing.

He had nothing.

And without Orchid, he really had nothing.

"Maine," she called, and he turned back despite himself. She ran up to him. "Wow, you're really deaf. I called your name three times."

"Thanks for reminding me." He started walking again, the almonds heavier than he'd anticipated.

"I'm sorry," she said. "I maybe jumped to some conclusions about you."

"Most people do," he said, wishing she'd been different. He really, really wanted her to be different.

"Maine, can you just stop for a second?"

He did, his teeth grinding together. "What?"

"Do you really like me?"

"Of course," he said. More than she knew. More than he knew, and that scared him a little bit. A woman in his life, especially one with a daughter, would change everything.

"Are you ready to retire?"

"Honestly?"

"I think we better be honest," she said grimly.

"No, I'm not ready to retire," he said. "Not right now. But guess what, Orchid? I don't have to leave the Orcas. They like me there, and if I go into the office tomorrow and ask for a five-year contract, I'll probably get it." He couldn't guarantee anything, but he certainly wasn't leaving next week. Or even next month.

Now next year....

Maybe.

But looking at Orchid standing in front of him, Maine knew that he wouldn't.

"Do you really want to meet my daughter?" she asked next.

"Of course."

"And you really want to open an ice cream shop?"

He stared straight at her, trying to decide if she found the idea ludicrous or not. "Yes."

Her face finally cracked as a small smile curved her lips. "What did you put in the fire to eat?"

"Potatoes and beets." He started walking again, his steps filled with much less anger now. "And you should know I've never cooked in a fire before, so they'll probably be half-raw."

Orchid giggled, and the sound tripped something in Maine. He paused again and lowered the almond bundle to the ground. "Orchid, I know I've said it before, but I'm going to say it again. I really like you." He gathered her into his arms, glad when she came willingly. "I went on that cruise hoping to meet someone," he whispered into her hair. "And I did. So things are changing. But that doesn't mean I don't want them to."

He pulled back and looked at her, almost desperate for her to believe him. "Okay? Can you understand that?"

"I'll try," she said, her voice high and tinny. "I'm trying."

"Me too." He leaned down and touched his lips to hers, a quick kiss that said almost as much as their more passionate ones under the waterfall.

They walked back to their camp together. Sure enough, the veggies were only done on one side, and Maine turned them while Orchid tried to wake up Tanner.

"He's not well," she said a few moments later. "I made him take some pills, but we've got to get him off this island."

Maine stared out at the water, wishing a boat would appear on the horizon.

Any minute now, it would.

Any minute....

Any minute....

Any minute....

CHAPTER ELEVEN

*O*rchid woke the next morning, the sunlight already bright and baking the day. She hadn't heard a rooster. Hadn't heard Maine when he'd gotten up and left the tree house. Hadn't heard Tanner do the same.

She sat up, alone in the shelter and wondering what time it was. She didn't like being alone, and she quickly ran her fingers through her hair, pulled it into a ponytail, and shimmied down the ladder to the beach.

Where she was also alone.

The fire smoldered, and she hastened to put another piece of the broken tabletop on it. If they didn't have to use another match today, that counted for something. She hoped.

She rubbed her hands up and down her arms, glancing around. Where had they gone? Tanner had looked a couple of steps away from passing out last night. Maine had helped him into the tree house early, and then come back to the fire, where he and Orchid talked and laughed softly, kissed and finally gone up to bed.

With the fire stoked and her hunger kindled, Orchid climbed back into the tree house just as a major squabbling sound lifted into the air. She darted to the back of the structure, where she and Maine usually slept, to see chickens lifting into the air.

They could fly for short distances, and something had clearly frightened these birds. A man yelled, and all at once, Orchid knew what Tanner and Maine were up to.

They were getting breakfast.

Her heart pounded at the continued yelling and squawking, but she decided she was glad she wasn't there. She didn't need to see death today.

Things quieted down, and she hurried to grab several potatoes and carrots, cradling them in her shirt so she could climb down from the tree. She walked through the hot sand to the water and rinsed them off, something Maine hadn't done the previous night. But she had no way to peel the vegetables, and she needed whatever nutrients they had anyway.

Back at the fire, she poked around with their fire stick to make a little section of just coals, and she nestled the veggies in to get toasty and soft. Only a few minutes later, Maine's voice could be heard, and she went to the path that led to the chicken meadow.

He laughed, his voice booming through the sky, as he came into view. Orchid's pulse hummed now, because he was so tall, and so good-looking. And she knew he had a good heart too—and he was carrying two chickens by their feet.

Catching sight of her, he beamed and started walking faster. "We got four chickens," he said proudly, holding them out as if she couldn't see them.

"Breakfast, lunch, and dinner," Tanner added from behind Maine.

"That's great," Orchid said, still thinking about how much wood they'd need to roast the chickens. Maine approached, and most of her cares and worries fled under the umbrella of his happiness.

"Hey, sweets," he said, drawing the dead birds behind him as he leaned down to kiss her. Orchid had never wanted to brush her teeth as badly as she did then. But she kissed him anyway, a little surprised he didn't seem to care about the display of affection in front of Tanner.

"Good job keeping the fire going," Tanner said, stepping past them. "Now we just have to figure out how to pluck these chickens and how to cook them."

Orchid pulled back and looked up at Maine. "Should I go get some wood to keep the fire going?"

"If you wait a bit, we can take the tarp and go together."

She pressed her lips together and nodded. "He seems to be doing better."

"He said whatever magic pills you gave him last night, he wants more." Maine chuckled, moved past her, and he and Tanner started discussing the best way to get breakfast in their bellies.

Orchid didn't particularly want to witness a beheading, and she did want fresh water for breakfast. Geared up with the backpack, the three bottles they had, and the bucket, she said, "I'll go get water. Be back soon."

"Okay," Tanner and Maine said at the same time, and she took the path that led more directly to the waterfall.

She didn't particularly like going off on her own, but she had the all-in-one tool in her pocket, and she knew the way there and back. It was a short seven-minute walk without the water, though she knew it would be harder and consume more energy on the way back.

She'd just filled everything and stuck the water bottles in her backpack when a growl sounded behind her.

Spinning, she kicked the bucket, spilling some of the water. But that didn't matter when she came face-to-face with a black boar, his long, white tusks the biggest she'd ever seen. Of course, she'd never seen an animal like this in real life. Didn't matter. The fear pounding through her was just as real.

She held out her hand like that would stop the pig from charging. He simply growled again, though the sound didn't sound like a dog or a cat or a lion. It definitely emanated from down inside the boar's throat, and it definitely made Orchid want to run.

Trying to keep her eyes on the boar and search for a way out of its path at the same time proved difficult. She finally gave up staring into the pig's beady eyes and scanned for an escape. The pool where she and Maine had gotten their water was enclosed with rock walls on three sides, with the waterfall at the back. If she could grab the backpack and sprint several yard to her right, she could jump up on a ledge there.

Orchid had no idea if pigs could jump or not. She knew they couldn't fly, so she bent slowly, her hand searching the empty air for the top of the backpack. She couldn't find it, and everything in her screamed at her to *run! Run now!*

Leaving the backpack behind, she sprinted for the rocks on her right, the squealing sound of the pig filling the air behind her, in front of her, everywhere.

She leapt, sure she was about to be gorged by boar tusks, and her knee and ankle wobbled as she landed on the ledge. She found her balance on both feet, her face only inches from rocks. She looked up and found another place to climb. She hadn't been outdoors much in years, but she managed to find enough foot and hand holds to get her up even farther.

Rocks crashed below her, but she refused to look down. It sounded like hooves on cement, and she didn't want to know if that boar could climb rocks the way she could. She simply had to out-climb it.

So up, up, up she went, her fingers bleeding and pain radiating through that knee and ankle that had taken the brunt of her weight when she'd jumped. She didn't care. She wasn't going to be pig food today.

Finally stalling when she couldn't find another hold, she took a deep breath and tried to calm the adrenaline raging through her. Only then did she realize how far up she'd climbed.

Looking down, the whole world spun. She slammed her eyes closed and gripped the rocks in front of her.

Then she screamed.

"I NEED YOU TO MOVE YOUR RIGHT HAND," Maine said from above her. "Come on, Orchid. I know you can do it."

But she couldn't. She'd already broken down on this stupid wall once, both Maine and Tanner watching her. They'd heard her scream, of course, and they'd both come running. They'd found a way to the top of the bluff, where Maine wanted to build a fire to signal ships, and with their help, she'd managed to move up the wall a little bit more.

"Just over a bit, sweetheart," he said. "And then up. There's a good hold there, and then I'll be able to get you." He looked at her earnestly, just out of reach. During her first breakdown, Tanner had offered to go back down and climb up the way she had, with the idea that he could help her back down. But he'd been thwarted in his efforts by a herd of boars—six, he'd yelled up to them—and was currently hiking back up to where Maine laid, one arm over the side of the cliff as he reached for her.

"I can't," she said, weeping again.

"Orchid, honey," he said. "Look at me. Look at me."

She tilted her head back and looked at him, but every angle besides looking straight ahead made a healthy dose of vertigo hit her.

"It's only over a few inches, Orchid," he said. "Then up about a foot. You have a good spot with your feet right now. You can do this." His eyes were wide, open, and honest. "Think about Tesla. You're going to be able to tell her how you scaled this huge bluff to get away from the boar. She's not going to believe it."

Orchid didn't believe it. She drew in another breath, choosing to listen to Maine's words *You can do this.*

You can do this.

Slowly, her fingers moved along the rock, going right and then up as Maine directed her. "Right there, sweets. Grab on." She did, and the hold was good. She felt stretched out, too thin, for too long, and she pushed off with her left foot, realizing too late she had nowhere to put it.

"Maine," she cried out, because she couldn't hang by her fingertips for long.

"Right there," he said. "Up a little more, almost on top of the right foot."

She found the ledge, which felt like it was about two inches wide, and straightened her leg. Pushing herself up, she was able to move her left hand high enough for him to grab it

"I got you," he said triumphantly. "Come on, Orchid. Another step, and you're up."

She looked down, found a spot for her right foot, and took it. Both of his hands clamped around her shoulders and pulled, and a few seconds later, she lay panting on the ground beside him, utterly spent.

She wasn't sure how long she'd been climbing, but it felt like a long, long time. She couldn't get enough air, and she closed her eyes against the hot sun and brilliant blue sky.

Maine started laughing, but Orchid didn't think there was a single funny thing about what had just happened.

She opened her eyes and twisted her head toward him. "Thank you."

He grinned at her. "Of course, sweets." He kissed her, got up, and helped her stand. "Now we just have to get back down."

"Tell me there's a path."

"I mean, sort of," he said. He put his fingers in his mouth and whistled, yelling, "Tanner. We're coming down. I got her," immediately afterward. He reached for her hand and squeezed it. "Stay with me, okay?"

"Okay." She kept her eyes on the ground, monitoring each step before she took it as they navigated their way back to the sandy ground. The pigs were gone, and the three of them collected the water and went back to their camp.

Orchid slumped against the tree trunk and drank an entire bottle of water while the men pulled vegetables out of the fire and rotated chickens. Soon enough, it was time to eat.

Orchid had just finished when Maine said, "Let's go get more wood. I'll grab the tarp, and we can go."

She didn't want to go get more wood. She wanted a hot bath. A toothbrush with a lot of toothpaste on it. Air conditioning. And a sink where water came out of a faucet.

Oh, and she never wanted to see a pig again.

Instead, she got up and followed Maine down the path that led to the chicken meadow.

CHAPTER TWELVE

*M*aine sat on the bluffs, able to see for seemingly ever. The first time he and Orchid had climbed to the top of the bluffs—without an angry boar snarling at their heels—he'd found the spot picturesque, calming, and beautiful.

It was still all of those things—except for calming. He'd spent hours and hours up here over the past four days, the absence of a rescue ship debilitating in a very real away.

Smoke lifted into the sky, as he and Tanner spent their time down on the sand cutting as much greenery as they could and hauling it to the top of the rocks. He had a three hundred and sixty degree view of the world here, and surely someone would be able to see the thick, white smoke as it billowed into the sky.

"Please," he whispered, his stomach cramping. He wasn't used to a dominantly vegetable and fruit diet, and while Orchid had taken over cooking the chickens he and Tanner caught so they weren't half-baked, he felt hungry almost all of the time.

At the same time, part of him didn't want to go back to real life. Practice schedules and paying bills and pretending to be the perfect role model on camera. Not that he wasn't a good role model. He knew he was.

But he sure had liked being real with Orchid for the past week. Footsteps sounded behind him, and he turned to see the woman cresting the bluff, her eyes trained on the ground so she didn't slip.

He smiled, everything in him rejoicing to see her. She was absolutely stunning, and his pulse picked up when she lifted her gaze to meet his. Even from thirty feet away, he could sense her anxiety and see the worry in her eyes.

Maine got to his feet and brushed off his shorts before approaching her. "Hey, gorgeous." His feelings for her were strong, and he sighed into their kiss.

She kissed him back in a pleasant, needful way, and he wanted to shelter her from everything that could make her scared or unhappy. He wondered what that meant. Wondered if he was in love with her.

Maine had never been in love with a woman before, and he honestly didn't know how it felt. But with Orchid...well, he didn't know.

"Tanner's freaking out a little," Orchid said as she laid her cheek against his chest.

"What is it this time?" Maine asked.

"He's convinced no one will ever find us," she said.

"I don't see how they can't," he said. "My parents won't stop looking. Will yours?"

She shook her head. "I'm sure Eden's spearheaded the rescue efforts." She stepped back and smiled up at him. "And your coach probably has every resource available at his command. Holden does, I know that."

"So they're just looking still," Maine said, facing the ocean again. "I didn't think we went that far off-course, but who knows with the storm and the tsunami." He couldn't believe he'd weathered both things, but he had. *They* had.

Orchid took his hand and squeezed. "Maybe today will be the day." She'd said that before—every day, actually—but Maine just nodded, like he always did.

"Maybe." He settled back onto the rocks, and Orchid sat beside him. He always wanted her there, and he leaned over and placed a kiss in her hair. "When I get back, the first thing I'm going to do is eat three hamburgers."

She giggled, which sent a shot of joy through Maine. "Yesterday it was five," she said. "And they had cheese and bacon on them."

"Hmm," he said, not amending what he'd said. "What about you?"

"Shower," she said. "I can't wait to stand in hot water and wash this trip off of my skin."

"All of it?" he asked, putting his arm around her.

"The killing chickens part," she said. "Sleeping with

115

a spear nearby, just in case. That part. Pulling up vegetables and getting insects." She shivered, and Maine swept his lips along her ear to her neck. "But maybe not all of it."

"Not me, right?" he asked, his voice throaty and low.

"Definitely not you." She turned toward him and claimed his mouth. Maine let her kiss him for a few moments, and then he drew everything out of her he wanted.

He pulled away breathless, his chest laboring, and said, "When *we* get back to Getaway Bay, I'm going to take you on a real date."

"Oh, I don't know," she said. "These secret bluff meetings are pretty hot."

He chuckled, shook his head, and looked out at the water again. So much water. Not enough hope to keep from getting drowned in the sheer enormity of it.

HOURS LATER—MAINE WASN'T EVEN SURE when—Orchid stood up and said, "Maine. There's a boat."

He'd laid back and closed his eyes, grateful for the tarp they'd erected into a lean-to on top of the rocks. It provided some shade and relief from the sun. Now that they had their food, water, and shelter situation worked out, they were literally marking minutes, and there was no better place for that than on the bluffs.

"Put more fronds on," she said, her voice panicked. "I fell asleep and the fire's almost out."

Maine recognized the urgency in her voice, though he was still trying to throw off the grogginess of sleep. "A boat."

"There's a boat," she said, a manic laugh following it. She tossed a couple of palm fronds on their fire, nearly putting it out.

"Don't smother it," Maine said, trying to help with the fire and search for the boat at the same time. He couldn't, so he focused on helping Orchid first. If there really was a boat, he'd have plenty of time to watch it approach the island.

He peeled back one of the fronds and lifted the other one, blowing on the embers at the bottom of the pile. They'd both fallen asleep at some point, and a stab of guilt touched his heart. Why hadn't he made sure the fire would last before lying down?

"How long have you been awake?" he asked.

"Five minutes," she said. "Maybe." She blew on the other side of the frond, and the flame ignited. "I'd just sat up and stretched. I stood up and took a few steps, just sort of casually looking. That's when I saw it."

She paused in the work of getting the fire raging again and looked out over the water. "It's still there."

Maine looked too, almost dreading it. What if she was wrong? What if her eyes were playing tricks on her? He'd stared at whitecaps plenty of times, imagining them to swell into yachts that would steam forward and rescue him.

But he didn't have to stare at something and allow it to morph into something it wasn't this time. He sucked in a breath. "There's a ship."

"I know." Orchid laughed again, this time the sound much more sane, and returned to the palm frond.

He lowered the second one, and it caught the fire pretty quickly. Thick smoke billowed into the air, and he straightened to watch the boat. After only a few minutes, it was pretty obvious that they'd seen the smoke and were coming straight for them.

Whooping, he grabbed onto Orchid and lifted her off her feet. Spinning, they laughed and laughed. He set her down and said, "Let's get out of here."

"What about the fire?" she asked.

"It'll burn itself out," he said, reaching for the tarp. He'd cut two sticks and stuck them between cracks in the rocks to keep the tarp up. Orchid had gathered loose rocks to hold down the back of the lean-to, but Maine removed them easily and balled the tarp under one arm while he reached for Orchid with the other. "Let's go, sweets."

He wanted to run down, but the path was treacherous, and he couldn't leave Orchid behind. It was about a forty-minute climb up and a thirty-minute jaunt down. By the time he and Orchid arrived at their camp, the ship had stopped.

It loomed large on the horizon, the best, brightest thing Maine had ever seen. Two lifeboats were in the water, rowing toward them, and Tanner stood in the surf about waist-deep.

Maine couldn't move toward the water's edge, the scene before him so surreal. Orchid had her pack. He had the clothes on his back. But for some reason, he wanted to climb into their tree house and get a few potatoes. A carrot. Maybe the spear he slept with. Something.

He couldn't leave everything behind, could he?

They'd killed two chickens that morning they hadn't eaten yet. It felt like such a waste. The boats came closer and closer, reaching Tanner, who climbed right in.

Orchid started for the shoreline, waving her arms as if the boats would leave without them.

Panic hit him in the chest, and he ran after Orchid, grabbing her arm and turning her toward him. "Things are about to change again," he said. "Promise me you'll call me."

"What?" She tore her eyes from the ship and looked at him, clearly confused.

"I'm going to have to be Maine Fitzgerald," he said, trying to make her understand. She'd see him differently, and if there was one person he didn't want to view him as the calm, cool quarterback, it was Orchid. "Please," he said. "What's your number? I'll call you."

Shouting came from the boats, and Orchid turned

toward them. "You promised me a date," she said. "You better call me." Then she ran down the beach again, yelling as she splashed into the water.

Maine looked back at the tree house. The remains of the fire where they'd cooked their meals for the past seven days. "Good-bye, island," he whispered, unsure as to why he felt a connection to this place.

Then he turned and jogged toward the water's edge too.

———

"I'M FINE," HE SAID FOR THE TWENTIETH TIME in as many minutes. But his coach was on the ship, and he'd brought three team doctors with him. One for each person, though Holden Holstein and his wife, Orchid's sister, were on the ship too, and they'd bustled off with Orchid and a doctor of their own.

"Dehydrated," one of the doctors in the room said. "Blood pressure elevated. He's lost some muscle mass."

Maine wanted to roll his eyes. He wondered if they had cheeseburgers on this boat. He hoped Orchid would get her hot shower—and that he could too. Getting poked and touched wasn't his idea of a fun time aboard a cruise ship, though this appeared to be more of a rescue vessel than anything else.

"Talk to me, Fitzgerald," Coach Bloom said. "What have you been eating? Not enough water?"

"I'm fine," Maine said again, appreciating his coach but not in the mood for this conversation. "I'm tired. No, the island didn't have steak and shrimp. We killed a couple of chickens each day. There was fruit, and an old garden someone planted."

"A garden?" Coach looked at one of the doctors. "People live there?"

"No." Maine shook his head and put on his media face. The one his public relations director had trained him to use. "It was an island where coast watchers lived during World War Two."

His coach looked like he'd been hit with a two-by-four. Maine knew exactly how he felt, especially as he got dressed in the suit his coach had brought for him. As he downed the protein drinks one after the other to get the doctors off his case. And when they pulled up to the docks in Getaway Bay to a mob of people, Maine actually did want to return to the island.

Instead, he put on his quarterback face and waved to the crowd. He caught sight of Orchid being escorted off the ship with her family, her head bent away from the cameras.

He wished he had that luxury. He wished he had her phone number. He wished not every question was being shouted at him, because there were two other people stranded with him on that island and their lives were just as important as his.

CHAPTER THIRTEEN

*O*rchid felt so much better after a good meal and a shower. Seeing all the people, all the cameras, hearing all the questions being yelled at the yacht sent her into shut-down mode. But she couldn't go there yet.

Her parents were here, and they had Tesla in the car with them. Eden had insisted she and Holden and Doctor Gimball be allowed on the rescue ship, and Eden herself had navigated them around to various islands. No one knew the islands better than Eden, and a rush of gratitude for her sister overcame Orchid again.

With Holden and Eden between her and everyone else, they managed to make a relatively quick and clean getaway from the ship. She glanced over her shoulder once to see a man wearing a suit and waving at the crowd.

It took her a long, drawn-out moment to realize it was Maine. But he didn't look like the Maine she knew, and all at once, his words on the beach made sense.

Things are about to change again.

I'm going to have to be Maine Fitzgerald.

She hadn't understood what he meant. But she did now.

They were from two different worlds. He couldn't be the Maine she knew. Her Maine Fitzgerald wasn't this polished, political man, and she barely recognized him in that suit, that fake smile on his face.

"They're right over there," Eden said, leading Orchid through the parking lot now, away from the crowds. Away from Maine.

Orchid followed, because the desperation to see her daughter and reassure Tesla that she was okay moved through her with the force of gravity. The back door on the SUV opened, and her towheaded little girl spilled out of it. "Mama!" She ran toward Orchid, who swept her daughter into her arms, tears flowing freely down her face.

"Hey, baby," she said, pushing Tesla's hair out of her face. "I'm okay. I promise. I'm fine." Eden had said she knew about the tsunami, the storm, and Orchid being lost out at sea.

"Were you scared?" Tesla asked.

"So scared," Orchid said. "But I'm fine. Look, I got you this shell." She pulled the seashell from her shorts.

"It's mostly intact. The waves on the island weren't as big as the ones here."

Tesla took the seashell and looked at it, flipping it over to see the shiny pink underside. She looked up at Orchid, whose knees were starting to hurt.

"And you won't *believe* this, but I climbed a rock wall. All by myself. And I learned how to cook chickens over an open flame, and—"

"Orchid," Eden said. "Let's get in the car, okay?"

Orchid straightened and followed her sister's gaze. People were coming their way, and she put her hand on Tesla's back. "Let's do what Aunt Eden says. Back to the car." She climbed in the very back with her daughter, leaving the middle seat for Holden and Eden.

She wanted to hug her parents. Cry until she had no tears left. Tell Tesla about the rock climbing, and the wild boars, and the vegetable garden.

About Maine.

She held everything in, the silence in the SUV as her dad navigated them through the mob and the cars to the exit, almost as unsettling as being on the island.

"We'll stop for food," her mom said. "And then you can tell us everything."

ORCHID EXHALED AS SHE PRESSED HER BACK into her bedroom door, the stories finally over. Her daughter had had a lot of questions, and her eyes had never been so round as Orchid told her all the things she'd done.

You really climbed rocks, Mama?

You really plucked and cooked a raw chicken, Mama?

You really helped that guy with his back?

She really had.

Even she couldn't believe it, but she felt a new strength inside her she wanted to hold onto. She wasn't the weakling she'd been when she'd boarded the StarMatch cruise ship. She'd spoken to people. Gone out of her comfort zone. Survived a tsunami strike, and then a tropical storm, and then seven long days stuck on an island.

She moved away from the door, the soft bed in front of her calling to her. She was so tired, even after napping on the ship. They'd only been eight hours from Getaway Bay, and she didn't have to sleep in a tree house.

Her parents had taken Tesla for one more night, and Orchid sank gratefully onto the soft mattress. Palm fronds and banyan leaves would never be this soft. Another sigh slipped between her lips.

She had no idea where her phone was. She thought she'd left it on the first ship, so it was probably at the bottom of the ocean by now. That ship could be anywhere, and she supposed she could try to call the company in the morning and find out what had happened to it, and if she could get her personal belongings.

If she had a phone, she could call. Which she didn't.

"Doesn't matter," she whispered to herself, stripping off all her clothes and climbing into bed. Sleep should've claimed her instantly, but she found herself awake, thinking about Maine.

She had no way of getting in touch with him either, and now that she was back in her comfort zone, back in Getaway Bay, in her home where everything was neat and organized and made sense...a relationship with Maine didn't.

With those thoughts in her head, she finally slept. When morning came, it was still fairly dark outside. Orchid pulled herself from bed and into the shower, staying in the hot spray for what felt like a very long time.

She wanted bacon cheeseburgers too, but at barely seven o'clock in the morning, she couldn't get one. She flipped on the TV as she started making coffee, a simple luxury she wouldn't overlook again.

Gratitude filled her heart as the newscaster said, "And now, we have the amazing story of the rescue of Maine Fitzgerald, starting quarterback for the Getaway Bay Orcas. We welcome him and the head coach of the team, Coach Jerry Bloom, to the show."

Orchid spun, her heart hammering out of control. Maine looked like the plastic version of himself, and annoyance filled her. No one had contacted her for an interview, and this star quarterback had glazed over when they'd arrived on the island. *Orchid* had got them all moving, and when Tanner got hurt, Orchid continued to get things done.

"Tell us," the woman said. "What was it like out there?"

"It's...vast," he said. "A lot of hopelessness. A lot of introspection."

"Not a bad answer," Orchid said, wishing she were on the set so she could give her answer to that question too. Kiss Maine afterward and tell him how great he'd done.

She would've said, *It was what it was. We were very lucky to have fruit and vegetables and wild chickens. When my sister was stranded on Bald Mountain Bluffs, they had nothing for a long time. So if there was an island to be stranded on, we got a good one.*

"What kept your hopes up?" the newscaster asked, and Orchid leaned closer to the TV, as if that would help her hear better.

"My team," Maine said without a moment's hesitation. "I went on the cruise with one of the wide receivers, and I knew Shane would be rallying everyone and everything he could." He glanced at Coach Bloom. "And I knew Coach wouldn't just carry on without me."

Coach Bloom smiled, but Orchid's chest had gone cold. Sure, Maine had talked a little bit about his teammates and his coach while out on the island. A very little bit. He'd told her more about his family, more about his dreams to open an ice cream stand, more about *him*, than anything related to football.

But it was his team that had kept his hopes up?

She scoffed and shook her head. "What a joke." She couldn't help the pinch of hurt that moved through her either. *What about you?* a tinny voice cried inside her mind. He'd said a couple of times he was glad she was with him. Glad they'd met on that singles cruise. Glad they were going through this together.

Was that all a lie? Another of his plastic personas? Another time when he had the exact right words to say and said them?

Orchid didn't know what to think. She didn't like the negative thoughts swirling in her head, but she didn't know how to banish them either. She looked at the screen again, disliking this version of Maine she saw.

He'd said he wanted to meet Tesla, take her out, have a relationship with her. Was any of that true?

"We've seen a few couples get stranded together in the past couple of years," the female newscaster said. "You were out there with a woman. Was there a love connection?"

Everyone chuckled, Maine included. He dropped his head and shook it. "I mean, I survived, you know? We all did what we needed to do. Tanner got hurt, and we took care of him. We worked together. We helped each other. There's a bond there, sure. I'm just glad I wasn't alone."

Orchid pulled in a tight, tight breath and held it. *I'm just glad I wasn't alone.*

Anger moved through her, and she hit the power button on the remote to turn off the TV. She got up from the couch, the scent of coffee telling her everything was set for the morning. But she couldn't stand still. Couldn't sit down.

Her hands shook as she poured herself a cup of coffee. She stirred and stirred and stirred, those words swirling the same way the brew did.

I mean, I survived.

He would've never survived without her and her backpack of supplies. It was *her* knife, her cord, her tarp, her desalination kit, her fire-starting kit that had saved them.

"*I* saved us," she said fiercely to herself. "Eden's foresight saved us."

Disgusted, she tossed the mug of coffee into the sink, the shattering of the ceramic startling her. Her emotions came down as she realized what she'd done, and before she could move to clean it up, the front door opened, and Tesla said, "Mama!"

She turned to hug her daughter, refusing to let any tears fall today. She was safe. She was home. And Maine didn't deserve her tears.

"Hey, baby," she said to her daughter.

"Do you want to go to breakfast?" Tesla asked. "Aunt Ivy said she'd pay."

Ivy walked in then, her phone held to her ear. She held up one finger and finished her conversation before saying, "So. Bacon. Eggs. Waffles. Let's go." She scanned Orchid. "You've definitely lost weight, and I *need* to hear everything about this quarterback you cuddled with on the island."

Ivy had been at Orchid's last night, along with the rest of the family, as Orchid had told the tale of the last several days. She'd mentioned Maine Fitzgerald of course, but nothing about holding his hand, or kissing him, or sharing parts of herself with him she hadn't with anyone since Henry.

She rolled her eyes. "There was no cuddling," she said, and she actually thought it sounded true.

"Mm hmm," Ivy said. "Get some shoes on. I'm starving, and I'm sure you are too."

CHAPTER FOURTEEN

*M*aine hated that the first face he saw as he walked off the set was Clarissa's. She'd spent hours with him last night too, and he just wanted to be left alone. His family had flown in from Texas, though, and they wanted to spend the day with him.

The morning news wanted a special feature, and Clarissa had begged him to take it. "It's good press," she said. "You're a local hero. Everyone loves you."

So he'd done it. He hadn't anticipated the love connection question, and his answer burned the back of his throat.

If Orchid saw that…he'd tried to warn her he wouldn't be allowed to be the same man she knew from the island.

And she wouldn't want him anymore, he knew that. He didn't even like this version of himself.

"You did great," Clarissa gushed. "You looked professional and personal at the same time. Our comment feed is full of well-wishes."

From females, Maine knew. But none of them actually wanted to know him. They had false ideas about him, about who he was, because of news spots like the one he'd just done.

Exhaustion pulled through him. "Do I have a new phone yet?" he asked when he should've told Clarissa thank you.

"Bobby's getting it this morning," she said. "After you spend the day with your parents, we have a six p.m. meeting with the owner. Bobby will have it for you then. All set up." She smiled like Maine should be so happy he had an assistant to set up his phone for him. Like it was hard.

His head hurt, as he'd slept for only five hours the night before. And with an evening meeting with Walt on the horizon, Maine didn't think he'd get to bed much before midnight either.

He just wanted to be alone.

On the island, he hadn't ever wanted to be alone. What a difference a day made, as well as the company he was with.

Clarissa walked off the set with him, and thankfully, his father emerged from an SUV parked in a drop-off zone outside the TV station.

Relief hit Maine right behind his breastbone. "Dad," he said, hugging his father fiercely. His dad had never been overly emotional. He'd driven Maine to work hard in school and on the football field, and he'd driven thousands of miles to watch his son play the game they both loved.

He said nothing, but when Maine finally stepped back so he wouldn't get squeezed to death, he could see the emotion in his father's eyes. "We've been so worried," he said. "And then they wouldn't let us see you last night."

"I'm okay," Maine said, looking behind him to the SUV. "Where's Mom? Honey? Diana?"

"At the resort," he said. "I was told I *might* be able to see you, so I didn't want them to come if we couldn't."

He glanced at Clarissa, annoyance filing him from top to bottom. "I'm free until the meeting tonight, right?"

"Yes, sir." If she felt bad about how the communication with his parents had gone, she didn't show it.

"Let's go, Dad," he said, walking around the front of the SUV without a backward glance at his public relations specialist. Sometimes he really, really hated being in the public eye.

But with the doors closed and the SUV moving away from the station, Maine leaned his head back and sighed.

"Breakfast?" his dad asked. "There's a great little place we found a couple of days ago. Private, on the beach." He glanced at Maine.

"Sure," Maine said. He didn't care where they went. He just wanted to eat, and private sounded really great.

His father let him lapse into silence as he drove over to the Sweet Breeze Resort and Spa.

As they approached, Maine wanted to ask his dad something before they got the rest of the family in the car. "Dad?" he asked. "How do you know when you're in love?"

His dad jerked his attention to him, his eyes searching Maine's when they should've been watching the traffic. "Maine...."

"I don't know if you saw the interview just now," he said. "I didn't want to say anything on TV. Her name is Orchid Stone, and I think I might be in love with her."

"The woman from the island?"

"Yeah." Maine looked out the window. "If she saw that...she won't even talk to me." Why had he said that? Why couldn't he have just been honest? "I don't know why I didn't want everyone to know about us. I should've just said, 'Yeah. Orchid and I are still getting to know each other, but I hope I can find her number and ask her to dinner.'" He looked at his dad to find him grinning.

Maine didn't know what he had to be so happy about. "Why didn't I say that?"

"I don't know, son. Why didn't you say that?"

"Because I don't want my personal life splashed all over the news."

"Well, that's not the professional life you have."

Maine didn't answer, because his father was right. And Orchid wouldn't want her personal or professional life all over the front page or in Internet articles either. And she'd never let Tesla be dragged into that.

Maine felt like a relationship with her was beyond his reach. If the media knew about it, they'd want to interview her. There would be cameras at her house, taking pictures, people asking questions.

Orchid wouldn't want any of that, and she'd be livid if Tesla had to endure it.

He sighed, wishing he'd met Orchid at a party or a restaurant, though he knew he never would've seen her at the same places he hung out. She was so unlike the other women he'd dated, but so much the kind of woman he wanted.

"Look, if you like this woman and you think the relationship is worth pursuing," his dad said. "Then do it. Who cares what the press says? You've never cared all that much before."

"Yes, I have, Dad," he said quietly. "That's why I have Clarissa. To make sure I don't screw up publicly."

"Falling in love is not screwing up," his dad said, turning into the driveway at Sweet Breeze. They'd barely pulled up when his mom and sisters came out of the building. Maine hastened to get out of the SUV then, his throat closing so fast he could barely say, "Mom," past the emotion.

He hugged her, the best feeling in the world getting embraced back by his petite mother. His sisters made a group hug, and he could hear one of them sniffling. Probably Honey. She was definitely the most emotional of the women in his family.

"Ma'am," someone said, and Maine stepped back from his mother. "You can't record this."

He watched as the valet took a woman's cell phone and started tapping. "I'm sorry," he said as she started to protest. Two security guards came through the doors, and the valet started explaining what had happened.

"Sorry," one of the burly men said. "He's right. We don't allow recording on the premises of people you're not with." He glanced at Maine, who gestured for his family to get in the SUV.

He managed to turn back amidst the woman's shrill protests and say, "Thank you," to the security guard and the valet. He closed the door and said, "Let's go to breakfast," at the same time his father said, "Maine fell in love with Orchid Stone on the island."

"Dad," he said as his mother shrieked and both of his sisters gasped.

"What? It's true." He eased away from the curb as the questions started flying, and Maine wasn't sure if he should be glad he had the chance to talk about it or annoyed at his father.

The truth was, he was a little bit of both.

"SO WHAT ARE YOU GOING TO DO?" HONEY asked. They'd spent a long time at breakfast while Maine told them about everything that had happened on the deserted island. Then they'd rented kayaks and gone to the beach, where he currently sat with his older sister under an umbrella. His parents were out in the ocean, and Diana had gone up to the shops to get something for her boyfriend back home.

"About what?"

"About Orchid, silly." She kept her sunglasses-covered eyes out on the water, and Maine appreciated that.

"I don't know." He'd been toying with dozens of options, from going to every flower company on the island until he found her to waiting to see if she'd come to him to announcing his retirement on the news the next morning.

"Do you really love her?"

"I honestly don't know," he said. "I've never been in love, Honey."

"Sure you have," she said. "You love football. You knew that was what you wanted to do. So when you think of the next year, or the next five years of your life, what do you see? Is Orchid there?"

He didn't have to think very long or very hard. "Yes," he whispered.

"Then you're in love with her," Honey said. "And you said some stupid stuff this morning. Big deal. Everyone says stupid stuff. Blame it on Clarissa. Whatever. But you better figure out how to make things right with Orchid, or you could lose her." Honey did look at him then. "I know, Maine. Remember when I screwed things up with Tyrone?"

"I remember," he said, reaching over and squeezing his sister's hand. "But he's back now, right?"

"He's back," she said. "We're working through things. That's all a couple can do. We love each other, and we're working through hard things."

Maine thought about the hard things he and Orchid had already accomplished together. He'd loved working alongside her, listening to her talk about her daughter and the school projects she did. "So what do I do? Show up at her house and ask if she saw the news this morning?"

"Yeah, why not?" Honey asked. "I followed Tyrone to Corpus Christi and refused to leave his hotel room until he would talk to me. I apologized. I told him I loved him. I told him our son needed him. That *I* needed him. People want to feel loved, and women especially want to know you need them." She tapped the brim of her sun hat. "Take it from me."

Maine nodded, his thoughts swirling again. yes, Honey had hit a rough patch in her marriage a year or so ago. Her husband had left for a few months. But they were making things work.

Maine could make things work with Orchid too. He'd done hard things before, both on the football field and off. "I don't have her number. I don't know where she lives."

"Her brother-in-law isn't hard to find," Honey said. "Right? Didn't you say he owns Explore Getaway Bay? Let's go there, and you can demand to call her sister." Honey stood up as if she'd drive him there right now.

"Now?" he asked.

"What are you waiting for?"

"It's four-thirty," he said. "I have a meeting with the owner of the Orcas in an hour."

"Ninety minutes," Honey said. "How long do you think a phone call takes? You get the info you need now, go to your meeting, and get Orchid back by morning." She beamed down at him. "Now come on."

Maine knew better than to argue with his sister. He also didn't want to stay away from Orchid or wait for her to come to him.

He got up and followed her, nervous the entire way over to the Explore Getaway Bay headquarters, which she put in her phone to find. Inside the lobby, he stalled. "I don't know, Honey."

"I do." She marched on, going right up to the desk. "Hi, my brother here needs to get in touch with Eden Holstein. It's a matter of extreme importance."

The woman there looked from Honey to Maine, who took the last couple of steps and stood next to his sister. "Hey," he said, his whole chest trembling. "I'm Maine Fitzgerald, and I said some really stupid things on the news this morning. I need to find Orchid Stone, and Eden is her sister."

The woman's mouth dropped open. "I saw you on the news this morning. You're Maine Fitzgerald."

He nodded, this woman's reaction fairly typical for him. "Yeah, I said that. Didn't I?" He looked at Honey and smiled before turning back to the receptionist. "Would it be possible for you to put me through to Eden Holstein? I'll stay right here and talk to her."

"That won't be necessary," a woman said behind them, and Maine turned to find another blonde standing there, oh-so-familiar though he'd never met her in person. "I'm Eden Holstein. Did you need something?"

He gaped at her until Honey elbowed him. Then he strode toward her, his hand extended. "Hello, Eden. I'm Maine Fitzgerald, and I'm in love with your sister."

CHAPTER FIFTEEN

"*I* don't want to go out tonight," Orchid said, holding her new phone to her ear with her shoulder while she washed her lunch dishes. Tesla had gone back to school, but Orchid still had a few days before she was scheduled to return to Petals & Leis. Her singles cruise should've still been going strong, and she felt so removed from that time. From that person she'd been before boarding the ship.

"Come on," Eden said. "You're slipping back into oblivion, Orchid."

"I am not," she said. "I'm doing fine." Better than ever, in fact. She'd started looking into what it would take to finish her nursing degree. She'd started a long time ago and being out on that island and needing some medical skills had reminded her how much she enjoyed taking care of others.

When she served others, she didn't have room to

focus on her own problems. And really, hers were first-world problems like running out of hot water because Tesla spent too long in the bathtub in the morning or opening the fridge to find they were out of chocolate milk.

Her sister sighed loudly into the phone, but Orchid didn't care. "I've been eating out for every meal since I got back," she said. "I already put a roast in my slow cooker, and I'm staying home tonight."

She knew the sacrifices her family, Eden especially, had made for her over the years. She often went along with most of what they wanted. But the fact was, she wasn't the same woman she'd been even two weeks ago.

It had been twelve days since the tsunami. Eleven since the storm. Three since she'd been home. Maine had not attempted to contact her, as he only seemed to have time for interviews and reunions with his family.

She couldn't begrudge him that, and she knew her obsession with searching the Internet for any news story about him was unhealthy. And yet, she couldn't seem to stop herself from doing it.

"What will it take to get you to the steakhouse?" Eden asked.

"Why is this so important to you?" Orchid asked. "If you want to come over, come over. I'm not going to stop you. There'll be plenty to eat."

"It's not that."

"Well, I'm not getting a babysitter so I can go to

dinner with you and your husband." Orchid turned off the sink and held the phone properly, a kink forming in her neck. "You don't want me there anyway."

Scuffling came through the line, and Eden said, "I have to go, Orchid. Talk to you later." The line went dead a moment later, and Orchid practically threw the phone into the sink. But last time she'd started tossing things around, she'd broken her favorite coffee mug. She'd just gotten this phone, and she didn't want to buy a new one.

Squeezing it extra-hard, she let out some of her frustration that way. Tesla wouldn't be finished with school for a few more hours, and then Orchid would have something to fill her time with. The insane idea to drive by the Getaway Bay Orcas sports complex ran through her mind—again. She'd been thinking about going there early in the morning and parking, waiting and watching to see if Maine showed up.

Surely he would. He'd been sequestered by his coach and personal trainers the moment he'd stepped up onto the rescue yacht. He'd said he wasn't due to show up for training until after the cruise, but the storm had changed everything.

"Absolutely everything," she murmured to herself, staring out her back windows at the water in the distance. She'd always loved this view, because she and Henry had bought this house for its spectacular view of the ocean out these windows. Tesla loved the beach and the ocean, and when Orchid couldn't take her, they could stand here and at least see it.

She turned away, having had her fill of the scene before her. At least now she had indoor plumbing just down the hall.

But she didn't have Maine.

His words from the beach rang in her ears. *Promise me you'll call me.*

She wasn't sure how he'd expected her to do that. Then he'd said he'd call her. She wasn't sure what she was supposed to do. She knew she missed him terribly, and she wanted his strength in her life. She wanted his reassurances. She wanted to share her fears and her triumphs.

Deciding she had to be the Orchid from the island the way she wished he was, she grabbed her keys and headed for her car. The Orcas had built an indoor training facility on a corner of the stadium property, and she knew that was where all the administration efforts for the team took place.

Maine might even have an office here. He was their starting quarterback. Maybe he had a dressing room the way celebrities did. She wished she'd had the foresight to ask him during one of their many conversations on the island.

As it was, all she could do was walk into the building and glance around like a tour guide would appear out of nowhere. No one did, and only the hum of the air conditioning overhead met her ears.

The building had been open, so she assumed she could go wherever she wanted. A museum of sorts sat to her left, and she went that way. The Getaway Bay Orcas were only a few years old, but there was obviously plenty of paraphernalia to fill the room. Trophies and medals, jerseys, shoes, and signed footballs.

She came to a life-sized picture of Maine himself, that cocky smile on his face. She stared at him, trying to find the man she knew within his face. He was there, that shy smile taking over his arrogant one. That handsome face as he looked at her and considered what she'd suggested. Those strong arms that held her at night.

Her heart pinched, and she didn't know what to do to stop it. She'd fallen in love before, and it had been wonderful. She'd never doubted her feelings for Henry, nor his for her. They'd been married quickly and spent only several months together before she'd become pregnant with Tesla and he'd died.

That kind of heartbreak she wouldn't wish on anyone, but at this moment in time, she felt all kinds of new cracks inside her chest, all originating in her heart. They spiraled out, infecting everything, and a sob gathered in the back of her throat.

She left the building without seeing anyone, thankfully, and drove to the elementary school, the first car in the pick-up line because she was so early. Didn't matter. She could take a nap here or search for more news articles quoting Maine. Why she wanted to torture herself with those, she wasn't sure.

Nothing new popped up in her search, and she ended up laying her chair down and closing her eyes. She woke when Tesla opened the door and said, "Mom, guess what?"

"What?" She sat up, her mouth feeling like someone had stuffed it full of cotton.

"We had an assembelbly. An assemelly—"

"An assembly," Orchid said, raising her seat to the right position to drive.

"Right. It was the football team you and Grandpa like. They did all these cool tricks."

"Really?" Orchid said, her heart beat skipping over itself. "What kind of tricks?"

"Not really tricks," she said. "They threw footballs into baskets and stuff. They never missed. It was fun."

"Hmm," she said, pulling into the line to get out of the drive-through lane. "What else did you do today?"

"We had mashed potatoes and gravy for lunch."

"Of course you did," she said. "It's Thursday." She smiled at her daughter. "And you're going to your watercolor class this afternoon. And swimming lessons."

"And Grandpa is taking me for sushi." She cheered, as Tesla loved sushi. Orchid did not, so she appreciated her father exposing Tesla to some things she simply didn't want to.

Orchid smiled at her daughter as she drove toward

the recreation center. Tesla usually rode an after-school bus there, but since Orchid wouldn't be back to work for a few more day, she got to do it.

She liked picking her daughter up after school. Liked listening to her talk about the things she'd done, and seeing her bright, full-of-life face right as she finished for the day. "Sweetie, I'm thinking about going back to school."

She looked at Tesla, who turned toward her with wide, innocent eyes. "I was studying to be a nurse when your daddy died. I'm thinking I'd like to do that again." She had no idea what it would take to do that, but she knew she couldn't work full-time at Petals & Leis. Maybe Burke would let her keep the job but allow her to work more flexible hours.

Determined now, she nodded at Tesla. "Things will change a little bit."

"That's okay," Tesla said, and Orchid wished for her childlike attitude.

She pulled up to the rec center and said, "Got everything?"

Tesla put her school backpack in the back seat and grabbed the bag she'd put there that morning. "Yep. 'Bye, Mom.

"Love you," Orchid said, watching Tesla get out of the car and skip toward the front doors. She joined another girl and her mother at the entrance, turning back to wave to Orchid one last time before disappearing inside.

Orchid sighed, put her car in drive, and went home. It was too quiet, and she hated being there alone. Maine's words from the interview suddenly made so much more sense.

I'm just glad I wasn't alone.

Well, Orchid *was* alone, and she didn't know how to remedy that situation.

A FEW HOURS LATER, JUST AS SHE LIFTED THE beautiful pot roast out of the slow cooker and onto her plate, someone rang the doorbell. It wouldn't be someone in her family, as they all just came inside whenever they wanted.

It was too early for Tesla to be finished with her activities and sushi, and besides her dad hadn't texted to say they were on their way home yet. He always did that.

Before, she might have been afraid. Tonight, though, she remembered she'd stared down a wild boar and then climbed fifty feet up a rock wall to get away from it. She could answer the door and not know who stood on the other side, just as she could look up what classes she still needed for her degree and open her application to the nursing program again—both things she'd done that afternoon after dropping her daughter off.

She crossed through the house, her stomach

rumbling for food, and opened the door.

Maine stood there, and he looked up from his phone, hastily shoving it into his back pocket. "Orchid," he said, and all the carefully crafted lies Orchid had been telling herself about him evaporated.

They just looked at one another, and she could see the man she'd fallen for right there in front of her. "You were right," she said.

"I'm sorry," he said.

"You had to go back to being a version of Maine Fitzgerald I didn't know."

"I don't know him either."

Orchid's pulse trembled through her body it rippled so fast. "How did you find me?"

"I tracked down Eden," he said. "I introduced myself to her, and I told her I was in love with you, and I needed her help." He smiled, but it was that hesitant, vulnerable grin she loved so much. "But she couldn't get you to the steakhouse. So I'm here." He glanced over her shoulder. "Something smells amazing."

I told her I was in love with you.

Orchid stared at him, no words coming to her mind.

"Can I come in?" he asked.

She still didn't move. "I'm sorry." She blinked and shook her head. "I need you to back up a little. You tracked down Eden, and…."

Maine looked at her with those eyes she loved so much. "I told her I was in love with you." He took both of her hands in his. "Because Orchid, I'm madly in love with you. I—love—you. I don't want to do anything without you. I actually *can't* function without you. I'm quite pathetic, but I'm trying to hide that until you take me back."

Orchid gazed up at him. "You said you were just glad not to be alone on that island. You've never mentioned me at all." She didn't want to show him he'd hurt her, but she'd never been great at hiding how she felt.

And he should know anyway. So she pulled her hands away from him and backed up a step.

CHAPTER SIXTEEN

*M*aine watched Orchid close herself off to him, the same way she'd done at the Battle of the Sexes Trivia night.

"I know," he said. "And I have a good explanation for that."

"I bet you do." She folded her arms and cocked her hip, and Maine's blood only ran hotter at the sight of her.

"I didn't want to put you in the public spotlight like that," he said. "Not without your permission. Do you realize what would've happened to you, your family —*Tesla*—if I'd said we were dating?"

She opened her mouth and shut it again.

"Maybe I should've said something," he said. "I don't know. So much of those interviews came from my public relations specialist, and I don't know." He exhaled, because he really didn't know. He knew he'd had to earn Eden's trust and that had taken a day or so. He knew he'd been frustrated since the moment he'd stepped foot back on this island. He knew he needed to earn Orchid's love and trust—and then Tesla's. And he was willing to do whatever it took to do that.

"You rescued me," he said, his voice almost breaking. "I actually miss the island, because I could just be me, and you were just you, and I loved her. I loved the me I was out there. I want that again, and the only place I'm going to find it is with you." He nodded behind her. "Can I please come in? I feel like all of your neighbors are watching."

She backed up, and he went inside her house and closed the door. "Thank you." He took a deep breath, getting the scent of that delicious meat, with the floral undertones of Orchid's skin. He knew that scent well.

"I saw your reunion with your mother and sisters," she said.

He growled and glared around at the house, because he wasn't really angry with her. "That was exactly the type of thing I was trying to protect you from," he said. "My private life isn't very private, and we never really talked about that out on the island. I don't know if you —you might be uncomfortable with that, and you should get to choose if you want me—and everything that comes with me—in your life."

There, he'd said it all. He'd followed his dad's and Honey's advice by finding Orchid. He'd done what Eden had said and led with how much he loved Orchid.

He'd done what he felt was right, and that was telling Orchid the absolute truth.

"I love you," he said again. "And I'll do whatever you want me to do, even if that's leave and never come back." His whole heart rejected that idea, but he couldn't force her to choose him.

She had to *choose him*.

She looked at him, and he felt very much like she was evaluating him with those eyes that missed nothing. "I don't have hamburgers," she finally said. "But this pot roast is pretty stellar, and the potatoes weren't cooked in a fire. If you want to stay for dinner, I wouldn't mind."

Maine chuckled, the laughter growing when Orchid finally smiled too. She giggled, and in the next moment, she launched herself into his arms. He caught her as she wrapped her legs around his torso and cradled his face in both of her hands.

"I love you, Maine," she whispered, looking down into his face.

"I can't believe it," he said, though every cell in his body tingled and told him she was telling him the truth. "I mean, I can believe it, but I can't."

She smiled that wonderful warm smile she had and leaned down to touch her lips to his. Maine thought he'd experienced the greatest kiss of his life under that waterfall on the island, but he'd been wrong.

This one with the woman he loved—and who loved him back—was a thousand times better.

"SHE'LL BE HERE ANY SECOND," ORCHID SAID, pacing from the front windows back to where he sat on the couch. Until her father had texted a few minutes ago, Maine had been holding her and kissing her and telling her about his meeting with Walter Germaine, the owner of the Orcas. He'd asked to be kept off the trading list, and if the Orcas ever found they didn't want him to play for them anymore, he'd retire.

Simple as that.

He loved his football career, but it wasn't going to be the focus of his life forever, and he knew that.

A moment later, the front door opened and a little girl burst through it. "Mama!" she called, coming to a stop a few feet later. "Oh, there you are. Look at this." She thrust a piece of paper at Orchid while Maine stood up from the couch.

The blonde girl looked a lot like Orchid, but her hair was much lighter and she had the eyes of her father.

"You're Maine Fitzgerald," she said, those eyes widening. "You came to my school today."

He had gone to an elementary school that day, as part of the team's community outreach program. "Hello," he said, hoping he didn't sound stupid. He knew how to deal with his nephew, and he hoped Tesla could be talked to like normal person.

Orchid flinched and looked up from the blue piece

of paper her daughter had given her. "This is great, Tesla. You're moving on to level three."

"Right?" Tesla asked, looking back at Orchid. "What's he doing here, Mama?"

"He was stranded on the island with me," Orchid said. "Remember Aunt Ivy told you that? He's the quarterback." Orchid moved over next to him and laced her fingers through his. "Tesla, he's also my boyfriend. Maine Fitzgerald, this is my daughter, Tesla Stone."

"Boyfriend?" Tesla's eyes got really big then. She gestured for Orchid to come back over to her, and she exchanged a glance with him before she did. She bent down and got on Tesla's level.

"Do you kiss him?" she whispered, but it was definitely loud enough for Maine to hear.

He chuckled as Orchid stage-whispered back. "Yes, Tesla. I kiss him."

"Gross," Tesla said with a giggle. She skipped the few feet to him and said, "Nice to meet you," and stuck out her hand.

Maine took it and shook it, this little girl creeping right into his heart. "And you, Tesla. Your mother's told me a lot about you."

"Yeah? What did she say?"

"She taught me that chickens can't swim," he said. "Because of a science...thing you did."

"Report," Orchid supplied for him, but Tesla had grown animated again.

"They can't swim. I mean, they can, but not for very long."

"Yeah, we saw that on the island," he said.

"Were you scared on the island?" she asked, and Maine crouched down in front of her.

"You know what, Tesla? I was. It was frightening sometimes. But I wasn't alone, and I learned a lot about how to take care of myself and what to put first in my life. So yes, I was scared. But I'm actually glad it happened."

She searched his face, and then turned back to Orchid. "Can I go get my report to show him?"

"Sure, sweets," she said, and Maine straightened and met her eye.

"Sweets?"

She shrugged. "I kinda like the nickname." She smiled at him and tipped up onto her toes. "She likes you, Mister Famous Quarterback."

"How can you tell?" He slid one arm around Orchid's waist and kept her close to him.

"I just know."

"Hmm." He kissed her, pulling away before he would've liked when little girl feet sounded in the hall behind him.

"*Y*ou have the ring?" he asked Tesla for probably the fifth time.

"I have it, Maine," she said without looking away from the window.

He was so nervous, but he couldn't wait another day. He'd already put off his proposal a few times now because of nerves, and he wasn't doing it again. Christmas would be here soon, and he wanted to celebrate with his fiancée.

"All right," he said, pulling up to the office building that had a huge Petals & Leis sign above it.

Orchid had put in her two weeks notice and today was her last day at the company. In January, she started back to school full-time. Maine's season had ended, and the Orca's hadn't made the playoffs for a fourth year in a row. He wasn't surprised, actually. They had some good new blood coming in, and maybe next year would be different.

"So we've got the cake and the ring," he said. "We should be set." He'd enlisted Tesla's help with the proposal, as he and the girl had been getting along so great in the afternoons when he picked her up.

"Do you think my mom will say yes?" she asked, finally looking at him.

"I sure hope so."

"What if she doesn't? Will you stop picking me up?" Tesla looked at him with a hint of fear in those pretty eyes.

"She's not going to say no," he said, confusing even himself. "She'll say yes."

"So you'll be my dad."

"I hope so," he said again. "You want that, right, Tesla?"

She nodded. "Yeah, I want that." She smiled at him. "So we'll just make her say yes."

He chuckled, his nerves getting the best of him. "That's not how it works." Reaching for the door handle, he added, "Come on. Let's go ask her." He collected the cake from the back seat, and they went into the building together.

Orchid's cubicle was up on the fourth floor, and he and Tesla rode in silence. The fourth floor was in full party mode when they arrived, and he put the cake on the table and kissed Orchid hello.

"There you are," she said. "I wondered when you'd get here."

"Here we are," he said, looking around for the source of the music. It came from a laptop on a nearby desk, and he stepped over to it and turned it off. "Everyone," he said, his voice strong despite the war currently raging in his gut. "I have something to say about Orchid."

"Oh, no," she moaned, but she had a flirty, fun smile on her face.

He waited for people to turn toward them and quiet down. "Well, it's not really a toast," he said, trying to find where Tesla had run off to. "But a question."

She appeared and handed him the ring box. "Thank you, sweets," he said to her. "Orchid, Tesla and I have a very important question." He met her eye, but she dropped her gaze to that little black box in his hand in the next moment.

"Maine," she warned.

"I love you," he said. "And I want us to be a family." He took a step toward her, glad when Tesla came with him. "Will you marry me?"

"Say yes Mama," Tesla said, looking between them. "Maine, you didn't even show her the ring."

"Oh. Right." He opened the box and held it up. "Will you marry me?"

Orchid started crying and nodding, and Maine's joy shot through the roof. "Yeah? Is that a yes? I can't quite hear you."

"Yes," she said, placing a sloppy kiss on his mouth. A cheer went up from her co-workers, and Maine turned back to all of them. "She said yes." He bent down and grinned at Tesla. "She said yes, sweets."

"She said yes!" Tesla started dancing around the office.

Maine turned back to Orchid, who wiped her cheeks. "I love you," he said, holding her close and kissing her properly.

"I love you, too," she whispered amid the chaos, and he hoped he could have moments exactly like these for the rest of his life.

Read on for a sneak peek at the final book in the series, THE SAND BAR MISSTEP to see if Ivy will be able to make a love connection with an Internet ad that takes her to a deserted island...

SNEAK PEEK! THE SAND BAR MISSTEP CHAPTER ONE

*I*vy McLaughlin bustled around the boutique, the new maxi-dress coverups tempting her. If she bought one, the money would come right out of her paycheck. She'd barely even miss it. Of course, she'd bought that crop top last week and a new pair of boyfriend jeans just yesterday. At the rate she was going, she'd be lucky to even get a paycheck on Friday.

So the swimming suit coverups went on the rack, despite her desire to take a size small in black to the dressing room and see how it looked with her newly bleached hair.

Everything about Ivy was new and improved. It had to be now that she was back on the market after a long relationship with Brooks Dentin—which had ended last week.

And she'd been so sure he'd asked her to the

fanciest fish house on the island to propose. But he'd gone all *Legally Blonde* on her and broken up with her. Ivy wasn't in a sorority, nor did she have any inclination to go to law school.

She just needed a new manicure. A new haircut and color. A new pair of jeans—*check*—and a new outlook on life.

Then she'd be fine.

Never mind that all of her sisters had now found love with some great guys. Eden and Holden were married now, as were Iris and Justin. Orchid and Maine would have an "event of the century" on the island by the end of the year, and Ivy was happy for all of them.

Honestly, she was.

She just wanted her own knight in shining armor. Or a football helmet. Or a Navy SEAL uniform. Or whatever. Since she'd been dating Brooks so seriously, she hadn't been calling in favors like she usually did to keep her social calendar full.

And now that she had access to the starting quarterback of the Orcas, she found she didn't want him to set up a date for her.

She wasn't sure what that meant, as Ivy was usually the life of the party. The star of the show. The one who turned heads, who could flirt with anyone with a Y-chromosome, the one who never stayed in on the weekends.

Now, she didn't even *want* to go out.

She felt broken inside, and she had no idea what to do about it.

Her phone rang, and she swiped on the call from her sister. "Heya, Eden," she said. "How's life in the glass building?"

"Just grand," Eden said, an edge to her voice that Ivy usually didn't hear unless Eden had good news.

"What's up?" Ivy turned toward the door as a chime sounded and watched two women walk into the shop.

"I have some exciting news," Eden said.

Ivy knew what her sister was going to say before Eden's voice landed in her ears. "Holden and I are expecting."

So maybe Ivy hadn't put those exact words in that exact order. A shriek had already started building beneath her vocal chords, and she let it out for just a moment. There was nothing better than being an aunt.

"I'm so excited for you guys," she gushed as the women came closer. If her boss was here and found her talking on the phone while there were customers in the store, he'd be furious. "Look, I have to go, but I'll call you back as soon as I can."

"Okay," Eden said, and Ivy hung up.

She approached the women. "Hey, ladies. Can I help you find something today?"

"She needs a new bathing suit," the brunette said.

"I do not," the other woman said. She threw her friend a scandalous look and tucked her regular brown hair behind her ear.

"Something sexy," the brunette said without missing a beat.

"Shannon."

"What?" Shannon asked. "You do. She's going to meet a guy out on this deserted island, and she wants to look hot for him. *Hot*. H-O-T."

"Stop it," the other woman said, actually reaching up and covering Shannon's mouth with her hand. "Just a regular bathing suit. I like a solid color. Black or red—"

"A solid color?" Shannon gasped as if her friend had just committed a fashion crime. She flipped a few more hangers on the rack in front of her, which didn't even hold swimming suits.

"We have some great one-shoulder stuff back here," Ivy said, hoping to draw the friend away from Shannon. "I've got solids and stripes." She really wanted to hear more about this deserted island. Maybe there was a singles event going on she hadn't heard about.

She'd been out of the singles scene for so long now, and part of her didn't want to get resubmerged in it. But summer had just arrived in Getaway Bay, and that brought a lot of vacationers out to the beaches.

Not only that, but summer was the best time to meet a new man, and Ivy felt some of the scales she'd been carrying for a while fall from her eyes. She could find a new boyfriend. She could.

She just didn't want to.

The island had plenty to do in the summer, and as

she pulled a black suit off the rack and held it out to the woman, she asked, "Where are you going to meet this guy?"

"Haven't you heard?" Her blue-green eyes sparkled with a secret. "There's this *crazy* billionaire who's put out an Internet ad." She rolled her eyes like the very idea was stupid. And yet, she was going to buy a sexy swimming suit to meet him. "He bought an island, and—"

"A deserted island," Shannon inserted.

"A deserted island," the woman continued. "And he wants someone to come live on it with him for three months. See if they can fall in love." She sighed like it was the most romantic thing in the world.

Ivy's heart started pulsing in her chest. At first, the sensation felt strange, as she hadn't felt anything like this in a while. Even while dating Brooks these last few months—which should've been a dead giveaway to her that their relationship wasn't going to last.

"She'll try that teal bikini too," Shannon said, and Ivy got it down amidst protests from the other woman.

"Come on, Kari," Shannon finally said. "You're going to meet this guy on his island. You can't show up in Bermudas and a T-shirt with a popsicle on it." She all but shoved her friend into the dressing room, another fistful of very revealing swimming suits in her hand.

Ivy smiled at the pair of them, their banter and back-and-forth so much like hers and Iris's. A pang of missing hit her hard when she thought of her twin. No, they couldn't stay together forever, but Ivy had always been so close to Iris, and she had Justin now.

The retired Navy SEAL worked for an app company now, and Ivy wondered if maybe he knew some single guys she could go out with.

Nope, she told herself as she picked up her phone from the check-out counter. She wasn't going to ask for help to get a date. Not this time.

No, this time, she was going to look up this crazy billionaire who'd bought an island and put out an ad for a companion. After all, money could make up for a lot of things. Maybe even a little bit of mental instability.

———

THAT EVENING, IVY SAT AT HER COMPUTER, the cursor blinking in the empty chat box in front of her. She'd read all about Mason Martin and his scheme to find someone to spend his life with.

His words, not Ivy's.

He claimed to be from Texas, and his proposition was clear. Come to Long Bar Island, about two hours south of Getaway Bay, and spend three months there with him. See if a love connection could be made.

The end.

He wouldn't be compensating anyone, and the only way he'd send out pictures was if someone messaged him and asked.

So Ivy sat in front of the chat box, ready to ask. Any time now. "Any minute," she muttered to herself. Beside her on the desk, the small guinea pig she sometimes took out and carried around with her lay curled into a ball.

If she went out to Long Bar Island, she'd have to figure out what to do with Tommy.

"He's a guinea pig," she told herself.

She'd been talking to herself all afternoon since looking up the email order bride scandal that had Getaway Bay in a twitter. She wouldn't miss anyone's birthday. She wouldn't miss Orchid's and Maine's wedding. And Eden had said she wasn't due until the first week of January.

Ivy had her job at the boutique, but honestly, it was exactly that—a job. Not a career. If things didn't work out with this Mason fellow, she'd come home and find something else to do.

She couldn't *believe* she was even considering this. There were singles cruises and beach parties right here on the island.

"Hello," she said as she typed out the words. "My name is Ivy McLaughlin. I've read your proposal, and I think I might be a good fit."

She read over the words again, and then again. She didn't want to ask for a picture of him right up front, though she could admit that looks were important to her. What if he was some sort of Quasimodo, and she didn't know it until her boat landed on the island?

"It's not all about what he looks like," she reminded herself, her hand hovering above the mouse, which already sat on the send button. She wondered how many people had sent him messages. Did he walk around the island? Maybe she could meet him that way.

Because this just felt ridiculous.

Her doorbell rang, and she jumped. Her knees hit the pull-out tray that held her keyboard, and her hand hit the mouse.

Moving quickly, she got up and hurried to the front door, adrenaline streaming through her now. "You ordered sausage and anchovies?" The guy standing on her porch with her pizza couldn't be more than sixteen.

"Yes." Ivy took the pizza from him and handed him the twenty-dollar bill on her front table. "Thanks."

"No problem, ma'am." He saluted—actually saluted her—and turned to leave. Disgust coated her insides.

"Ma'am." She was only thirty-one-years-old. She wasn't a ma'am. Was she? "It doesn't matter," she told herself as she took her food into the kitchen. "He was way too young for you."

Something beeped from her computer, and she turned toward it. The machine sat just outside of the kitchen, back toward the front door. Another beep sounded, and a box popped up as she watched.

"Oh, holy starfish," she said, abandoning the food as she sprinted back to the computer.

She'd sent her message to Mason Martin when

she'd been startled by the pizza delivery guy. And he was responding. With pictures.

He had dark hair and dark eyes, and he looked downright good enough to eat. His broad shoulders met Ivy's requirements, and she could only imagine what he'd look like out on an island with his shirt off.

"He's handsome," she murmured as another image came up. Another box ticked. Rich. Good-looking. So he wasn't Quasimodo. Hopefully, he wouldn't be the Beast either.

Most people want to see what I look like, he'd typed. *That's me. Mason Martin. I'm 35.*

Are you from the island? Ivy typed into the box, all thoughts of eating now gone, because this man was checking her dating requirement boxes faster than she could think of what they were.

THE SAND BAR MISSTEP is available now in ebook and paperback!

The Perfect Storm (Book 1): A freak storm has her sliding down the mountain...right into the arms of her ex. As Eden and Holden spend time out in the wilds of Hawaii trying to survive, their old flame is rekindled. But with secrets and old feelings in the way, will Holden be able to take all the broken pieces of his life and put them back together in a way that makes sense? Or will he lose his heart and the reputation of his company because of a single landslide?

The Overboard Mistake (Book 2): Friends who ditch her. A pod of killer whales. A limping cruise ship. All reasons Iris finds herself stranded on an deserted island with the handsome Navy SEAL...

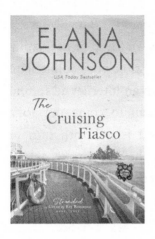

The Cruising Fiasco (Book 3): He can throw a precision pass, but he's dead in the water in matters of the heart...

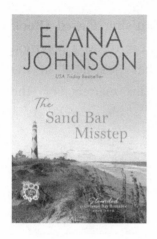

The Sand Bar Misstep (Book 4): Tired of the dating scene, a cowboy billionaire puts up an Internet ad to find a woman to come out to a deserted island with him to see if they can make a love connection...

The Island House (Book 1): Charlotte Madsen's whole world came crashing down six months ago with the words, "I met someone else."

Can Charlotte navigate the healing process to find love again?

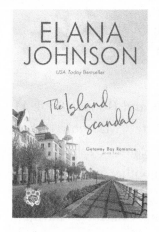

The Island Scandal (Book 2): Ashley Fox has known three things since age twelve: she was an excellent seamstress, what her wedding would look like, and that she'd never leave the island of Getaway Bay. Now, at age 35, she's been right about two of them, at least.

Can Burke and Ash find a way to navigate a romance when they've only ever been friends?

The Island Hideaway (Book 3): She's 37, single (except for the cat), and a synchronized swimmer looking to make some extra cash. Pathetic, right? She thinks so, and she's going to spend this summer housesitting a cliffside hideaway and coming up with a plan to turn her life around.

Can Noah and Zara fight their feelings for each other as easily as they trade jabs? Or will this summer shape up to be the one that provides the romance they've each always wanted?

The Island Retreat (Book 4): Shannon's 35, divorced, and the highlight of her day is getting to the coffee shop before the morning rush. She tells herself that's fine, because she's got two cats and a past filled with emotional abuse. But she might be ready to heal so she can retreat into the arms of a man she's known for years...

The Island Escape (Book 5): Riley Randall has spent eight years smiling at new brides, being excited for her friends as they find Mr. Right, and dating by a strict set of rules that she never breaks. But she might have to consider bending those rules ever so slightly if she wants an escape from the island...

The Island Storm (Book 6):
Lisa is 36, tired of the dating scene in Getaway Bay, and practically the only wedding planner at her company that hasn't found her own happy-ever-after. She's tried dating apps and blind dates...but could the company party put a man she's known for years into the spotlight?

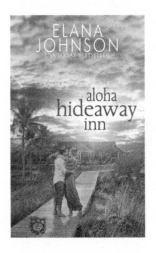

Aloha Hideaway Inn (Book 1): Can Stacey and the Aloha Hideaway Inn survive strange summer weather, the arrival of the new resort, *and* the start of a special relationship?

Getaway Bay (Book 2): Can Esther deal with dozens of business tasks, unhappy tourists, *and* the twists and turns in her new relationship?

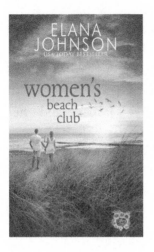

Women's Beach Club (Book 3): With the help of her friends in the Beach Club, can Tawny solve the mystery, stay safe, and keep her man?

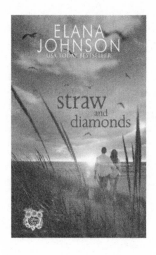

Straw and Diamonds (Book 4): Can Sasha maintain her sanity amidst their busy schedules, her issues with men like Jasper, and her desires to take her business to the next level?

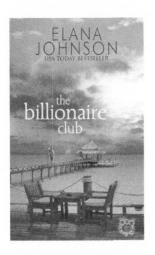

The Billionaire Club (Book 5): Can Lexie keep her business affairs in the shadows while she brings her relationship out of them? Or will she have to confess everything to her new friends...and Jason?

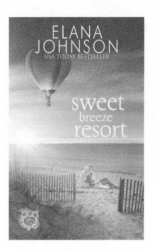

Sweet Breeze Resort (Book 6): Can Gina manage her business across the sea and finish the remodel at Sweet Breeze, all while developing a meaningful relationship with Owen and his sons?

Rainforest Retreat (Book 7): As their paths continue to cross and Lawrence and Maizee spend more and more time together, will he find in her a retreat from all the family pressure? Can Maizee manage her relationship with her boss, or will she once again put her heart—and her job—on the line?

Getaway Bay Singles (Book 8): Can Katie bring him into her life, her daughter's life, and manage her business while he manages the app? Or will everything fall apart for a second time?

The Day He Drove By (Hawthorne Harbor Romance, Book 2): A widowed florist, her ten-year-old daughter, and the paramedic who delivered the girl a decade earlier...

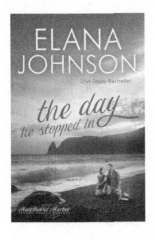

The Day He Stopped In (Hawthorne Harbor Romance, Book 3): Janey Germaine is tired of entertaining tourists in Olympic National Park all day and trying to keep her twelve-year-old son occupied at night. When longtime friend and the Chief of Police, Adam Herrin, offers to take the boy on a ride-along one fall evening, Janey starts to see him in a different light. Do they have the courage to take their relationship out of the friend zone?

The Day He Said Hello (Hawthorne Harbor Romance, Book 4): Bennett Patterson is content with his boring firefighting job and his big great dane...until he comes face-toface with his high school girlfriend, Jennie Zimmerman, who swore she'd never return to Hawthorne Harbor. Can they rekindle their old flame? Or will their opposite personalities keep them apart?

The Day He Let Go (Hawthorne Harbor Romance, Book 5): Trent Baker is ready for another relationship, and he's hopeful he can find someone who wants him and to be a mother to his son. Lauren Michaels runs her own general contract company, and she's never thought she has a maternal bone in her body. But when she gets a second chance with the handsome K9 cop who blew her off when she first came to town, she can't say no... Can Trent and Lauren make their differences into strengths and build a family?

The Day He Came Home (Hawthorne Harbor Romance, Book 6): A wounded Marine returns to Hawthorne Harbor years after the woman he was married to for exactly one week before she got an annulment...and then a baby nine months later. Can Hunter and Alice make a family out of past heartache?

The Day He Asked Again (Hawthorne Harbor Romance, Book 7): A Coast Guard captain would rather spend his time on the sea...unless he's with the woman he's been crushing on for months. Can Brooklynn and Dave make their second chance stick?

ABOUT ELANA

Elana Johnson is the USA Today bestselling author of dozens of clean and wholesome contemporary romance novels. She lives in Utah, where she mothers two fur babies, works full-time with her husband, and eats a lot of veggies while writing. Find her on her website at feelgoodfictionbooks.com

Made in United States
North Haven, CT
25 January 2024

47895421R00125